FOOTSTEPS
IN THE OCEAN

FOOTSTEPS IN THE OCEAN
Careers in Diving

Denise V. Lang

LODESTAR BOOKS E. P. DUTTON NEW YORK

Copyright © 1987 by Denise V. Lang

Library of Congress Cataloging in Publication Data

Lang, Denise V.
  Footsteps in the ocean.

  "Lodestar books."
  Bibliography: p.
  Includes index.
  Summary: Discusses career opportunities in sport and commercial diving, underwater science and research, and underwater military operations.
  1. Diving, Submarine—Vocational guidance—Juvenile literature. [1. Diving, Submarine—Vocational guidance. 2. Vocational guidance] I. Title.
  VM984.L36 1987 627'.72'023 86-28725
  ISBN 0-525-67193-5

Published in the United States by E. P. Dutton,
2 Park Avenue, New York, N.Y. 10016,
a subsidiary of NAL Penguin Inc.

Published simultaneously in Canada by
Fitzhenry & Whiteside Limited, Toronto

Editor: Rosemary Brosnan

Printed in the U.S.A.   W   First Edition
10 9 8 7 6 5 4 3 2 1

For Larry, my dive buddy, my friend, my husband, who gave me the gift of the undersea world. And for Chris and Tiffany, the next generation of divers to leave footsteps in the ocean.

CONTENTS

ACKNOWLEDGMENTS

A book as ambitious in scope as *Footsteps in the Ocean* could not have been produced without the generous assistance of many outstanding professionals from the various diving disciplines.

I would like to give special thanks to Dr. Bruce Bassett, Human Underwater Biology; Don Chittick, Sea World; Jim and Cathy Church; William Dunn, *The Orlando Sentinel*; Dr. Sylvia Earle, Deep Ocean Engineering; Randy Hanks, Underwater Vehicle Training Center; Morgan Hardwick-Witman, Northeastern University; Lt. Robert Hayes, Harbor Unit, Underwater Recovery Team, New York City; Les Joiner, The Ocean Corporation; and Dr. Bert Kobayashi, University of California, San Diego.

Special thanks also goes to Daniel Lenihan, U.S. Parks Service; Dr. Bill Lindberg, University of Florida; Cinematographer Jack McKenney; Gary Parsons, Professional Diving School of New

York; Drew Richardson, Florida Institute of Technology; Ed Sala-mone, National Association of Scuba Diving Schools; Paul Tzimoulis, *Skin Diver* magazine; James Williams, Professional Association of Diving Instructors; and Dr. Jon Witman, North-eastern University. And to Christopher, Tiffany, and Larry Lang, without whose cooperation *Footsteps in the Ocean* would have never been written.

LEAVING FOOTSTEPS

Cool, salty waters flow silently through the maze of living corals and gently swaying grasses at the ocean's bottom.

Man, a funny-looking creature, air bubbles escaping above his head, glides through a school of colorfully arrayed parrot fish. No thoughts of earthbound responsibilities burden his mind. No sounds of telephones, automobiles, or human voices intrude upon the solitude and magical sights swelling his senses.

An idyllic scene, to be sure. And while man used to savor this serenity merely for pleasure, dwindling world resources, refined underwater techniques, and progressive scientific discoveries now lead him to leave footsteps in the ocean while pursuing a myriad of exciting careers.

Some clarification of terms is in order, for the terms scuba diving and skin diving are often used interchangeably. Actually, the two activities are quite different.

Skin diving refers strictly to the mask-fins-snorkel type of diving one can do in the colorfully alive waters of reefs or the unexplored depths of the backyard swimming pool. Air is supplied only through the snorkel. The skin diver's movements are restricted by the length of time he can hold his breath and the intensity of the waves surging over him.

Scuba diving takes its name from the equipment used: Self-Contained Underwater Breathing Apparatus. Scuba divers receive their air supply from tanks, usually mounted on their backs. In some commercial diving operations, air, or a mix of gases, may be supplied through long hoses attached to tanks fixed to the deck of a ship. The scuba diver's movements are restricted only by the air tank capacities or by hose length. With today's modern equipment, divers can explore the depths of the ocean, frolic with sea life, or conduct month-long research projects from specially pressurized habitats.

For purposes of this book, all diving referred to will be scuba diving, unless specifically stated otherwise.

Navy divers were the first to focus public attention on diving as a career during World War II. This career choice was limited, by definition, to those serving in the military and therefore excluded women. The first major developments in diving technology came about during the war, when hundreds of men were lost because of a lack of adequate amphibious training. The need for underwater demolition teams and the invention of efficient breathing apparatus made military divers unique. Training programs had been developed for them, but there was little instruction available to the general public.

The advent of television brought the show "Sea Hunt" into the nation's living rooms. Lloyd Bridges, as diver-for-hire Mike Nelson, doggedly pursued bad guys and recovered stolen gems from the bottom of the sea. Still, there was limited call for flamboyant underwater experts who specialized in rescuing lovely ladies or carrying out secret missions.

Jacques-Yves Cousteau, inventor of the Aqua-lung and renowned oceanographer, captured the imaginations of millions around the world while introducing us to yet another facet of underwater career choices. Who can resist the sight of that wiry Frenchman with his trademark red cap? Mesmerized, we sit before the television screen and watch as he explores the march of the tropical spiny lobster or the antics of nocturnal Arctic creatures. The adventurer in each of us is there with him until he once again rises to the surface.

Cousteau's brand of undersea exploration still represents only a fraction of the opportunities available today to men and women interested in diving as a profession.

The ocean, our planet's last frontier, offers challenges, excitement, and opportunities that are continually expanding. The three major categories of career opportunity in the diving industry are sport diving, commercial diving, and science and research. Each of these major areas can be broken down further into specific career opportunities.

To begin, everyone interested in diving for fun or profit, research or business, must learn to dive and receive a nationally recognized certification. The person who starts the process rolling is the dive instructor. The bond between instructor and student is forged out of a sharing in the mysterious world beneath the sea and the techniques necessary to enjoy an escape to that world.

As the ranks of sport divers swell by the thousands yearly, there is a growing need for dive masters and dive resort managers. Since relatively few are lucky enough to live in close proximity to the ocean year-round, divers must spend vacations trekking to resorts and dive destinations around the world. These are run by the dive master or dive resort manager who organizes dive trips and activities for visiting aqua-nuts.

Profiting from the ability to share underwater pleasures, the underwater photographer, writer-diver, and cinematographer also enjoy new horizons. There is a burgeoning focus on diving from publications and advertising agencies to filmmakers, and those in the creative arts are finding that diving skills greatly add to their marketability as well as their pleasure.

The sport-diving industry is rounded out by the sector that brings students and instructors together, educates the public on safe diving equipment and techniques, and provides the necessary equipment and dive trips to enjoy the sport—the retail business. Dive shops serve as centers for learning as well as for social gatherings. And the efficient use of computer technology has lifted the dive shop into the modern retail world.

While sport diving is usually the drawing card initially, many find commercial diving holds a certain appeal—it is one of the most highly paid areas in the industry. As major oil companies invest large sums of money and equipment to burrow ever deeper into the earth's crust, highly trained divers must be hired to perform construction and maintenance jobs. Commercial air divers and bell saturation divers are responsible for a myriad of tasks ranging from underwater inspection and photography to welding and mechanical repairs.

In addition, with more than three hundred U.S. and foreign nuclear power plants in operation today, the need for trained underwater maintenance crews is great. That number does not even include the thousands of hydroelectric power plants and inland waterway projects that also offer opportunities to the commercial diver.

A major technical breakthrough in the commercial diving industry has been the development of remotely operated vehicles (ROVs). These underwater robots can work at depths never before explored. They can remain underwater indefinitely to perform a variety of simple to complex tasks, indifferent to the human requirements of food, warmth, and rest. The need for technicians to direct them has opened a new career opportunity for the electronically minded diver. Remotely operated vehicles are also being employed for profit by salvage divers, who are now able to reach shipwrecks and industrial equipment in deep waters.

Although diving is simply a tool in science and research, marine biologists and ecologists view it as one of the most important, as it brings the scientist face-to-face with his subject matter. From the halls of universities to research centers to private consulting firms, marine biologists and ecologists are in demand not only to define life and food chains under the sea, but to make predictions and safeguard human food supplies. Marine pharmacology— deriving medicine from sea life—is another area of scientific research that is on the brink of expansion. And the very specialty of underwater archaeology owes its birth to the development of scuba equipment and, now, deep-sea submersibles. Imagine tracking a country's history from the fragments of pottery rescued from some historic wreck!

With more activity taking place underwater, with its unique atmosphere and attendant hazards, even the medical profession is expanding to include professionals and diver medics capable of handling problems indigenous to diving. Diver physicians and medics are needed for the commercial industry as well as for sport diving. Not only has specific training been designed for the medical group, but the profession has discovered that treatments formerly used only for divers have broad applications for other diseases.

Apart from these three major diving divisions are two more specialty areas that provide career training in diving. One is the military and the other is police search and recovery. Both have growing needs and training programs for highly skilled professionals.

The ocean floor is a little more crowded today than it was when Cousteau first pioneered the Aqua-lung, but it is as vast and deep as the possibilities for learning and development. Diving has been called the growth industry of the future. The "new pioneers" are finding that future is wide open.

FOOTSTEPS
IN THE OCEAN

1

DIVE INSTRUCTOR

They teach you the names for the equipment, how to make it work, and—miracle of miracles—how to breathe underwater.

They teach you how deep you can go and how to return to your world safely.

And, more than that, they hand you the keys to a world of beauty, bursting with life, color, and self-discovery.

Who are *they*? The dive instructors . . . the first-line representatives of the industry. They have the power to impress the interested, create new divers, and perpetuate the sport of diving.

Sport diving today is enjoying tremendous growth—an increase of more than 15 percent each year. A stable economy and the lack of competitiveness in the sport have made it a glamorous way to spend both money and leisure time. Its attraction as a family sport with some limitations (students must be fourteen years old to be certified) adds to its appeal. With this growth goes the demand for well-trained dive instructors.

But what are the qualifications to be an instructor? Do you have to be six feet tall, weigh two hundred pounds, be able to swim five miles without stopping, and then leap tall buildings in a single bound? Not at all. Although the original navy divers, who learned by the seat of their pants—and necessity—conjure up images of burly hunks capable of punching out sharks, today's instructor has changed to fit the times and clientele.

"The image of the macho instructor is going the way of the dinosaur," says Ed Salamone, associate director of the National Association of Scuba Diving Schools (NASDS). "In addition to teaching the basics of diving, today's instructor is selling romance, excitement, adventure—coming across the gold doubloon."

For that reason, experts agree that candidates for dive instructor are evaluated in terms of maturity, dependability, commitment, charisma, and personality. In addition, instructors must be able to not only handle groups of people in a foreign environment and maintain control, but they must be able to deal successfully with emergency situations.

Women, as well as men, are finding that the position of dive instructor offers opportunities outside the usual type of teaching post. The classroom is the ocean, and students attend because they are enthusiastic about learning. In fact, women instructors have been actively recruited by diving schools. While some men still find they are combating the old macho frogman image, women—according to school training directors—display a special sensitivity to a broad range of students and, in turn, become better teachers. A woman as scuba instructor also presents a less threatening image to a wide range of age groups. Teenagers can easily relate to her, female students are less intimidated, and men don't feel they have to keep up a superman image while struggling to learn something totally new.

While good health is a prerequisite for an instructor, unusual physical strength is not. Those entering the field should go through a complete physical examination, however. Some conditions that may prevent a successful diving career include heart disease, diabetes, sickle-cell anemia, chronic asthma, and weak knees, as instructors do a lot of underwater kicking as well as equipment hauling.

Most schools are delighted to start training those who have already been certified divers for a while, but all offer basic dive-instructor training to those uncertified as well. The most typical candidate for dive instructor is one who has been certified for a while and wants to make the sea a second home. He or she understands and appreciates the complexities of visiting that mysterious world and wants to share it with others.

Al Hornsby, vice president of the Professional Association of Diving Instructors (PADI), says that the decision to go into professional diving is generally aimed at achieving an alternative lifestyle. "The question that comes up is 'Am I going to just work? Or am I going to work at something that means something to me?' Virtually everyone in the industry has left something else to come into this field. Because the experience is so profound, working underwater is like going on a safari."

While basic instructor-training programs vary with the certification agency, prospective dive instructors may take a range of preparatory courses including equipment repair, retail operations, diver recruitment, search and recovery, underwater photography, and diving physiology. The objective of all training courses is to teach the prospective instructor how to teach others to dive, how to select the proper equipment, and how to handle the possible situations arising from a dive.

Concurrent with the power to teach and mold new divers is tremendous responsibility. Every time an instructor takes eight people diving, he or she has the well-being of eight lives in his or her hands. For that reason, anyone thinking about becoming a dive instructor should go through intense preparation including extensive study and practice in a variety of specialties.

Fortunately, there are a number of highly reputable organizations that offer instructor training at several levels of proficiency.

The YMCA, the National Association of Underwater Instructors (better known as NAUI), and Scuba Schools International (SSI) conduct training programs for dive instructors either locally or at regionally designated locations throughout the year. These associations depend heavily on affiliated dive shops for recruitment and training. In addition, each YMCA is totally independent, so programs, teachers, and affiliations may vary to accommodate individual geographic locations.

The National Association of Scuba Diving Schools and the Professional Association of Diving Instructors, the largest certification agency in the country, both have two-pronged programs. Interested divers can study under the auspices of a local dive shop and then attend an abbreviated course of instruction at organization headquarters, both of which are in California. Or if the prospective instructor is free to travel and can spend several months away from home, he can enroll in the formal Career Programs. These consist of more than 450 hours of training held at the associations' California campuses.

Because of the growing popularity of diving as a career choice, two universities offer combination academic degrees for students who train in the sport-diving field. The Florida Institute of Technology (FIT), located in Jensen Beach, Florida, provides a curriculum in which students obtain an associate degree in sport-diving operations, plus dive-instructor ratings from both PADI and NAUI. The University of California at San Diego offers diver certification up to master level as well as boating courses leading to a bachelor's degree in physical education. These programs, designed to fill a hole in the diving industry, prepare the student academically as well as provide a number of diving specialty courses.

Application information can be obtained by contacting your local dive shop or one of the schools listed in the appendix.

Once the instructor rating has been obtained, the possibilities for employment are wide open. From tropical resorts to Canadian dive shops, from YMCAs to the actual certification agencies themselves, the demand for qualified instructors is constant.

Schools such as PADI, FIT, and NASDS provide extensive placement assistance to their graduates. PADI even has a computer hot line that provides job descriptions for opportunities all around the world as they open up.

Then it's the instructor's turn to test his training and get to work.

A typical dive instructor will be associated with a dive-shop operation, either as a partner or simply as an employee. He or she will teach the basic dive-certification program from the agency that trained him or her. This usually includes a specified number of hours of classroom work during which the students are taught a little about diving physiology, marine life, the pieces of equipment to be used, and the "safe diving" code of behavior: "Always dive with a buddy" and "Plan your dive—dive your plan." A specified number of hours in a swimming pool follows, where the students become accustomed to donning and operat-

Dive instructors get their students accustomed to awkward equipment in a swimming pool before taking them into open water.   PROFESSIONAL ASSOCIATION OF DIVING INSTRUCTORS

8   FOOTSTEPS IN THE OCEAN

ing the equipment and learn emergency procedures and how to be a safe, knowledgeable diving buddy for someone else.

Teaching the step-by-step process of diving is really only the beginning. The dive instructor must fire the enthusiasm of his students while emphasizing the serious aspect of the sport. He then serves as administrator of the tests for certification and the judge of those tests. He must evaluate his students as divers and as dive partners for other divers.

Depending upon the instructor's own expertise and ratings, he or she may also conduct classes in advanced open-water techniques, cave diving, night diving, wreck diving, and classes geared toward the student's achieving an expert diver rating. The instructor will lead dives, listen to fears about sharks and sea monsters, and be privy to his students' first looks of wonderment at their glimpses of the underwater world.

The ultimate success of the dive instructor lies with his commitment to safe, quality diving; his ability to teach patiently; and finally, his willingness to assume responsibility for the lives of others.

◄ An instructor checks his student's pressure gauge to record how much air is available for the dive. PROFESSIONAL ASSOCIATION OF DIVING IN-STRUCTORS

2

~~~~~~~~~~~~

DIVE MASTER /
DIVE RESORT
MANAGER

Imagine waking up each morning to the sun kissing your face as palm fronds gently sway a greeting in soft, tropical breezes. Going off to work means putting on your bathing suit, trotting down to the old dive boat, and greeting six to ten enthusiastic divers ready to spend the day under your care.

With the sun blazing overhead, you—star of the show, master of knowledge—outline the dive sites you have selected for the day. Then off you go. Stories of diving adventures are exchanged on board, and soon you lead an awestruck group of happy followers through familiar reefs and colorful sponges forty feet below. On the ride home, everyone is on a first-name basis. Your charges ask your advice on equipment and express their gratitude for an exciting and fulfilling experience.

Back at the dive shop, you catalog equipment and, satisfied that you created the highlight of the week for your clients, look over the list of divers for the next day's trip. Oh, and don't forget you have a date to meet that charming couple from Europe for dinner.

A day in paradise? The perfect, glamorous job? Maybe. But the glamor carries a stiff price tag that may not be readily apparent.

What if the compressor that fills the air tanks breaks down while you are preparing your dive group for the trip and there's no repairman within two hundred miles? And the diver from Kansas, who has saved for a year for this vacation, begins letting you know how unhappy he will be if the dive is called off?

What if, instead of capable divers, you have two who have just been certified, two who haven't been diving in ten years but wanted to try again during this vacation, and one supermacho type who intimidates all aboard with his gruesome tales of taunting killer sharks and bloody barracuda?

What if a storm blows up and several divers turn green from being seasick? And what if one of the divers uses up all his air, panics, and tries to rip the air hose off one of the other divers at a depth of forty feet?

The job of a dive master / dive resort manager is full of "what if's." It is this facet of the job that necessitates thorough training in a wide range of specialty disciplines.

The categories of dive master and dive resort manager are lumped together here because, while some agencies and resorts consider them separate categories, very often the responsibilities and training overlap.

Technically, a dive master is the one on the boat who leads a dive with only certified divers. The dive master may or may not be the captain of the boat. The dive master may or may not also be a dive instructor or the dive resort manager, depending on the size of the resort.

Technically, the dive resort manager is simply the person who is in charge of the dive resort operation on land and has nothing to do with the actual in-the-water diving. In most cases, however, the dive resort manager also serves as the boat captain, dive instructor, and dive master.

While the title varies with agency and resort, the qualities and responsibilities are similar.

Pamela Balash, course instructor for PADI International College and former dive master / dive resort manager in the Virgin Islands, says one of the biggest assets of a professional in the resort business is a sense of humor and flexibility of skills. "You must be an optimist. Things can happen there that don't happen in the 'real' world."

That sense of real world versus the unreal world of the resort area prevails from the islands of Hawaii and the Caribbean to ice diving in the northern United States and Canada.

Self-sufficiency is the number-one requirement for a dive professional contemplating resort work. Training in equipment repair and maintenance is a must, because often resorts will not have access to repair people on a regular basis. Since diving is an equipment-concentrated industry, when the equipment is down, you are out of business.

Hospitality and a genuine liking for people helps both the dive master and dive resort manager. Because diving is also a *business,* it is as important for the dive master / dive resort manager to look as if he is really enjoying his work as it is for him to be trained in personnel management and marketing. A dive resort manager must combine the skills of an able hotel and business administrator with the love and understanding of diving. For that reason, schools such as FIT, PADI, NAUI, NASDS, SSI, and Underwater Careers International offer not only a range of preparatory dive courses in the dive master / dive resort manager rating but retail preparation as well. Those who do not have a business orientation should consider other alternatives.

Many dive-master courses include charter boat operations, ocean bottom topography, diver stress, rescue-diver certification, night and deep diving, and the teaching of the "resort course"—a very brief and basic instruction program for vacationers. All either require or include first aid and cardiopulmonary resuscitation (CPR) certifications in the rating.

One of the main challenges a dive master in a resort faces is

Explaining the underwater terrain and checking the experience of sight-seeing divers is part of a dive master's responsibilities. PROFESSIONAL ASSOCIATION OF DIVING INSTRUCTORS

the variation in quality of divers who wish to go on dive trips.

Jane Cambouris, who, with her husband, Peter, owns and runs one of Hawaii's more popular resort "dive destinations"—Central Pacific Divers on Maui—says that sometimes the dive master "winds up baby-sitting for divers who say they've been diving for two years, and then once they're down, it's apparent they have no experience. Some people will just outright lie about their diving experience." For that reason, her dive masters spend time talking with every diver on the boat prior to a dive and try to assess who may need extra help to ensure a safe dive.

Another facet of the more successful dive master's repertoire is his or her ability to "show and tell" underwater, says Cambouris. Knowing the underwater terrain and taking the time to pick

Hawaii's reefs and volcanic formations allow dive masters to introduce their divers to unique sights.   ROD CANHAM / CENTRAL PACIFIC DIVERS

up a small octopus and pass it around or feed a moray eel can make a dive a memorable adventure.

Health requirements for the dive master / dive resort manager, as for the dive instructor, are basic.

For those dive masters who are also assuming the additional responsibilities of dive resort manager, a good background knowledge of the politics and customs of the island or general resort area is necessary to successfully obtain work permits and direct tourists to other leisure activities.

A dive resort manager's day would typically include setting up a specific dive trip, explaining the trip to prospective divers, and then booking that trip. He or she also coordinates dive personnel and fun activities for both before and after diving. The dive resort manager is responsible for advertising the resort, selling equipment, and handling any problems that don't fall under the dive master's or dive instructor's sphere of influence.

"Even though this is your job, you have to remember that people are paying you for recreation, and they are probably bringing their everyday stresses and hostilities with them," says Pamela Balash. "It's a fine art to making diving fun, easy, and enjoyable and still stress the importance of safety to the student or recreational diver."

3

~~~~~~~~~~~~~~~~~~~~~~~~

DIVING JOURNALIST

When Paul Tzimoulis was just a teenager in the 1950s, his first diving experience was to put on a simple mask and flippers to search for the best bass-fishing spots in a Connecticut lake.

He thought it was so much fun that a few years later he became a scuba instructor and underwater photographer conducting classes for the YMCA. He went on to open a dive shop, become a sponge diver in Greece, a diving equipment salesman for various companies, and eventually a lecturer on his wreck-diving adventures and underwater photography experience.

But how to reach a broader audience? Write about it! And so he did.

Today, Paul Tzimoulis is the Petersen magazine group publisher of *Skin Diver* magazine, the largest water-sports publication for divers. He has led campaigns to save shipwrecks off New York, had lunch with an ex-cannibal, discovered the sunken

Paul Tzimoulis *(left)* interviews cinematographer Stan Waterman and author Peter Benchley *(right)* in Bermuda during production of the movie *The Deep.*   SKIN DIVER

remains of lost pirate ships, and located the remnants of an eighteenth-century British 101-gun man-of-war battleship. And thousands of diving enthusiasts have been able to share in these experiences through his colorful and detailed writing.

For many, the idea of diving and telling other people about it is the ideal job. And so it may be, but being a successful diving journalist requires careful study and proper training. However, there is no course of study leading to a degree in diving journalism. It is rather a combination of skills obtained through several sources and brought together under the common interest of sharing the undersea world with both divers and nondivers alike.

In the growing diving industry, there are many opportunities for those who want to get into communications, but the competition is fierce. The more skills one can offer, the better his chance of selling an article.

"In the diving journalism business, you really have to be a writer and a photographer," advises Tzimoulis. "The fact is that the market is looking for a package deal. Or find a collaborator whose skills complement your own, so you can still turn in a package."

Becoming a diving journalist is more than simply describing what you see underwater. The first preparation is a good education in both photography and writing. This can be accomplished either through a formal journalism program or creative writing classes in addition to diver training. Underwater photography courses are usually offered through local dive shops or by independent photographers. One can also prepare for a diving jour-

Paul Tzimoulis photographs a giant sea turtle off West Palm Beach, Florida. *SKIN DIVER*

nalism career through less formal means, but a great deal of practice is always necessary.

Secondly, the more successful diving journalists are involved in the dive industry through working at a dive resort, a dive-equipment company, a dive shop, or as dive instructors. This puts them in touch with the industry and the people who run it. It allows them to know what developments are occurring, identify emerging growth areas, and focus on popular resorts and new equipment.

The prospective writer should then study the market. If you wish to write an article on diving in the Bahamas, you have to be aware of what has already been written and which publications would be most receptive to another story on Bahamas diving. There are numerous diving magazines, both industry-related and recreational, as well as diving newspapers and newsletters that could offer possible opportunities for sales. Full-time employment as a staff writer on most of these publications is possible, but free-lance articles are the major source of copy in this forum. Tzimoulis recommends obtaining at least six copies of a publication to study its style and scope before trying to write an article for it. A list of publications about diving can be found on pages 128–129.

Unlike the regular journalist, who can research a subject about which he knows little, interview someone, and then write a convincing article, the diving journalist is dealing with a semitechnical field. The editors reading the prospective article are all experienced divers as well as editors, so the writer must know what he is talking about. You cannot fake making a seventy-foot dive to scour the ocean bottom, hoping to discover a wreck. There are too many technical variables, sensory experiences, and emotions that will not ring true to the editors or readers of your article.

Once experienced as a diver, and educated and experienced as a writer or photographer, the next step to becoming a published diving journalist is the query letter. In this letter, you will let the editor of the publication know what kind of article you propose to write, its approximate length, and the kind of pictures available to accompany it. You may suggest a deadline or leave that up to the editor. And you should include a list of credentials of both writing and diving experience.

Then comes perhaps the hardest part of all. You wait to hear if your query has piqued the editor's interest.

Monthly publications have a long lead time—that is, they work on issues three to five months in advance. Therefore, if you have an idea for a great dive-resort story, perfect for Christmastime, you should query monthly publications during the previous spring.

Many diving publications will be happy to send the prospective writer their list of guidelines for writing. Many publications have preferences as to whether you send photographs, slides, or transparencies or whether they accept color pictures or only black and white.

By obtaining this information at the outset, you will begin building a file that will allow you to present yourself as a professional when struggling to obtain assignments. It will also prevent you from wasting both your time and the editor's.

In compiling a portfolio of published stories, don't overlook local and regional magazines and newspapers. Very often, a local newspaper would love to have a story about a travel resort with the added flavor of the diver's viewpoint. Or, if your sheriff's department has a search and recovery team, the local newspaper may call upon you to write a news story or side feature, if you have already presented your credentials and demonstrated your ability to understand the technical aspects of diving.

The main thing is to keep trying.

4

UNDERWATER
PHOTOGRAPHER

It is 8:20 A.M., and the telephone rings in the office of one of New York's diving schools. An editor from the local newspaper is calling. He needs a photo to advertise a big fund-raising sale at the shopping mall and wants to use a diver in full wet suit as the attention-grabbing "prospective shopper." Can they send one over as soon as possible?

In California, a group of people has been on the beach for most of the day, shooting several ads for a watch company. They finally decide to head underwater and photograph a diver to emphasize the waterproof durability of their product.

And at a hotel in the Caribbean, the manager commissions an underwater photographer to take several underwater shots to be included in the hotel's brochure in order to entice a wide range of guests to his vacation spot.

Suddenly divers are emerging from the depths of the ocean to appear in ads selling boats and cars and wet suits and whistles —and everything in between. The country has discovered diving! Credit must be placed, in part, at the feet of underwater photographers, who have brought the world beneath the sea, with all of its color and intrigue, to the surface, enchanting people of all ages.

There are two primary avenues that an underwater photographer can take in pursuit of the perfect frame.

First is that of an employee of a dive shop, either stateside or in a resort area somewhere in the world. As a shop employee, the photographer may or may not also be a dive instructor and can earn his or her living selling underwater camera equipment and supplies, teaching underwater photography classes, or providing photographic services for guests and customers. Some dive shops offer the skills of an underwater photographer as a means of recording its customers' dives. The vacationer goes home, not only with stories about the fantastic sights underwater, but with photographs of himself as the star. What a way to impress his friends!

The underwater photographer may also find himself filling air tanks, selling diving equipment, or performing one of the many other jobs necessary to keep a diving operation going.

The second avenue is that of a self-employed, self-directed professional. This path requires that the underwater photographer carve out a career for himself. It is fun to fantasize about traveling from Hawaii to Bonaire to Australia, snapping photos underwater and then sending them to the welcoming arms of editors from *Skin Diver, Scuba Times,* or *Diver.* As in any of the arts, however, the photographer has to develop a name for himself. This takes time and exposure (no pun intended) and, until that independence is attained, the underwater photographer should have some other means of supporting himself.

Jim and Cathy Church, a husband and wife team generally recognized as two of the premier professionals of the underwater print media, live the fantasy. On a moment's notice, they can be called to shoot an ad in the Caribbean or do an article with photos in Kauai, Hawaii. It took nearly ten years of dedication to achieve this autonomy.

"Nearly everyone in the business had some vehicle to get their cameras in the water," says Cathy Church. "Al Giddings, whose work is now on television, was an engineer who then designed camera housings for underwater shots." Another photographer was a ship's captain who took photos while running dive tours, and yet another ran a travel service so he could go to exotic places, take his photos, and then try to sell them. The Churches were, and still are, teachers. "You have to carve out a niche for yourself and establish a need for your pictures."

The Churches' vehicle was their teaching. Jim, with a master's degree in business management, and Cathy, with a master's in biology, taught school full-time and spent summers and vacations taking underwater photos. They gradually decided to use their teaching skills to conduct underwater photography classes during their vacations. And from there, they progressed to writing articles for *Skin Diver,* illustrating the use of underwater camera equipment for the beginning underwater photographer. Ten years later, they were totally self-employed as a photo-journalism team.

"Editors now call up Jim because he's never missed a deadline and they know the quality of the work they are going to get," says Church, who has also served as underwater model and coauthor of the couple's books on underwater photography. "Editors like predictability. They want to know exactly what they are going to get and that they are going to get it on time."

Again, the marketability of a photographer's skills in the magazine arena depends upon his ability to both photograph and write. Editors look for photo-article packages on products and travel. Just as in the case of the diving journalist, the photographer must study the changing market to see what is needed.

While artistic ability is the focus for most photographers, attention must be paid to organizational ability. One can be a good

Cathy Church *(left)* instructs student in using an underwater strobe to highlight small marine animals.   JIM CHURCH

photographer, but if he doesn't meet deadlines, pay his bills on time, advertise his skills and classes properly, or maintain records, he will not make it in this highly competitive field.

The underwater photographer must not only be a good diver who is able to handle a camera expertly underwater, he must also be able to capture an experience, a scene, and a mood in a foreign environment—usually under the pressure of a deadline and with no excuses.

"Kids ask us about becoming underwater photographers and what skills they can practice. We ask them, 'Can you get your English paper in on time?' " says Church. "And if it isn't right, can you stay up all night to get it right and not come up with some excuse about being sick or family problems? Can you handle that kind of stress? If you can, then it's a good start."

A moray eel unwittingly strikes a pose for this underwater photographer off Florida's coast. FLORIDA INSTITUTE OF TECHNOLOGY

Magazine and periodical exposure provides only half the opportunity open to an underwater photographer. The other half is the underwater advertising market, which Church feels is the place today where a career can really take off. Again, the underwater photographer must be capable of handling a number of contingencies.

"We once got a call from a company that wanted both land and underwater shots. They wanted me in an all-yellow wet suit. I didn't even have an all-yellow wet suit. And we had one week to deliver the photographs.

"We've gotten in the water, and the fish wouldn't cooperate. We have been on sites where it was raining and the shots had to be in ideal tropical weather. You can't make excuses to the company," said Church. "It is the photographer's job to get himself to a site where he can make it happen."

"Making it happen" is indeed the byword of the underwater advertising business. Photographers may be given an assignment by people who know what they want in an ad but have no concept of what is involved in getting the shot underwater.

It is the responsibility of the underwater photographer to select the site, hire the models if necessary, organize and transport the proper equipment to the site, transport the ad people, make the travel and lodging arrangements, get everyone and everything back home on deadline, and then be good on every roll of film without fail.

Helpful skills include the ability to take orders and follow directions, even if you think the desired scene is wrong. You give the ad director what he wants, and if it is wrong, the burden lies with him. The wise underwater photographer will also shoot extra photographs that the director should have asked for. The director will be happier, and the photographer will be admired for his professionalism. The ability to negotiate diplomatically is an asset that allows creativity to sneak into a routine assignment.

Perhaps surprisingly, the underwater photographer needs a good understanding of math. Not only does he need to understand film speeds, camera angles, and light exposures, but he must also deal with water refracting the light, as well as "bottom time" diving tables and water pressure affecting both his body and his work.

Since this type of underwater photographer works on a schedule based on assignments, he does not keep regular nine-to-five hours. When an assignment needs to be fulfilled, he must be able to work long hours and maintain his health. It is not unusual to spend eight hours under water to obtain the proper shot required.

Finally, the underwater photographer must be able to take criticism. "The photographer must have the innate ability to see and interpret someone else's objective," says Church. "Sometimes that objective does not agree with the photographer's artistic impressions." But that interpretive skill plus an understanding of advertising layout and design, and an understanding of underwater creatures, will allow the underwater photographer to grow within the confines of the business-oriented discipline.

It all comes back to the ability to "make it happen" and the attitude that nothing is impossible.

"*Impossible* just means doing it right the second time," says Cathy Church.

5

UNDERWATER CINEMATOGRAPHER

Luck has been holding so far. The warm waters are clean, the stars of the movie—or their doubles—are in position on the wreck, which rests sixty feet below the surface, and the safety diver is out of camera view. The time to film is now. You give the hand signal to begin action on the fight scene and zoom in to get close-ups. Suddenly something whacks the back of your head. Grabbing the camera tighter to keep it from falling, you glance around in time to see a pair of hammerhead sharks gliding off to circle and make another pass. Drawn by human activity in their watery realm, they intrude silently once more, their lifeless eyes measuring you . . . for a snack?

Ah, another day in the life of an underwater cinematographer!

Hollywood has lured the hopeful for as long as the young have had dreams of stardom. And now, divers are following the song of the sirens to Tinsel Town as the television, video, and movie industries begin to incorporate underwater shots in their productions.

Someone has to be the first person in the water—the person behind the camera recording the stars' exploits and making it look as though they are the only ones in the water. That person is the underwater cinematographer.

While the opportunities are relatively few in number—if you compare it to the traditional work of camera operators—and the competition is stiff, underwater cinematography is a tremendous skill to add to the professional's repertoire of services in order to find employment in the movie industry. The more skills you have, the more you can offer a producer, and the better chance you have of finding employment.

There are three general areas of work for an underwater cinematographer: second-unit work, director of underwater photography, and producer of your own films.

Let's say the script for one segment of "The A-Team" calls for an underwater scene. The producer of the show will call in an underwater cinematographer to handle just that scene. "Here's the situation," he or she will say, "and this is what I want." The rest is up to you. That is second-unit work—producing an underwater sequence to be incorporated into a script that is not primarily an underwater show.

It is the underwater cinematographer's responsibility to assess equipment needs, select the underwater location best suited to the producer's desires, and hire all divers or peripheral help he will need for the actual filming. He must make arrangements to transport equipment and people to the dive site, shoot the scene, and deliver it into the producer's hands as a finished product on time.

Second-unit work is the most common form of underwater cinematography, and the pay is good. It is not, however, usually plentiful enough that one can support himself on it without other forms of employment. The second-unit cinematographer is an employee of the producer of the film who has contracted to turn in one small segment. His responsibility ends when he delivers his piece of film.

Director of underwater photography carries with it the excitement (and headaches) of being totally in charge of an underwater production. While second-unit work may mean one underwater scene, the need for a full-time director of underwater photography means the film has a large percentage of its scenes underwater. *Jaws* and *The Deep* are two examples of films requiring the services of a director of underwater photography.

The director of underwater photography must choose the location; hire the divers and cameramen; and gather, provide, and transport the camera equipment, which, in itself, is a challenging job. The need for twenty 110-pound boxes of underwater photographic equipment is not unusual. He is also responsible for making travel reservations for all concerned, hiring the boats, working with the costumers, and, finally, directing the actual shooting. Then everything and everyone must be transported back to shore and home again.

Finally, an underwater cinematographer can serve as producer of his own films if he is willing and able to provide the financial backing necessary for creating a film. Producing is a career that usually starts out as a hobby until a reputation is built in the business.

Jack McKenney has just such a reputation. He has worked as a stuntman and underwater cameraman for Cornel Wilde's *Sharks' Treasure* and doubled for Nick Nolte in the thriller *The Deep*. His work has appeared on all three major television networks, and he is the producer of many independent underwater films for both governments and private corporations. An author, lecturer, and former editor of *Skin Diver,* he is a frequent contributor to such publications as *National Geographic*.

His most dramatic job, however, was that of chief underwater photographer and cameraman for Peter Gimbel's TV special, "The *Andrea Doria:* The Final Chapter." It was during this proj-

Jack McKenney directs Norine Rouse and Raja the turtle in a film off West Palm Beach, Florida. BARRY PARKER

ect that McKenney also had his closest brush with death . . . and he wasn't even in the water.

"Three of us were in the four-ton diving bell being held up by a cable when the cable snapped. Fortunately, we came down on the deck of the mother ship. If we had still been over the side, we would have gone crashing down onto the deck of the *Doria,* 160 feet below, rolled off, and dropped to the bottom. The bell would have flooded, and chances are I wouldn't be here to tell the story," he says.

Is the underwater cinematographer's job a hazardous one, then?

"Sure there are some risks, but they're calculated ones," says

McKenney. "If you prepare well enough for it and understand what's required, the danger is minimal."

Preparation and *understanding* are the two magic words in a cinematographer's vocabulary. Preparation includes meeting the many challenges that separate topside cinematography from its underwater counterpart.

"You need a working knowledge of bodies of water, so you can get the producer what he wants," says McKenney. "You have to understand exactly what he is trying to achieve so you can give it to him.

"From a shooting standpoint, you may get to a location and have dirty water—that's a common problem and a big one. You can try and choose a location where you know the water's consistently clean, but a lot has to do with luck and the project.

"On the *Doria* project, we had only ten-to-fifteen-foot visibility at times. It was very dark. But for a documentary-type film, it can work. If you're doing something theatrical, though, and the picture calls for one-hundred-foot visibility, you can't have anything less. You have to go out and find it."

Keeping the photographic equipment dry is another challenge. Underwater cinematographers have to invest not only in quality cameras and support equipment, but also in the underwater housings—or cases—to keep them from getting wet. The cameras, housings, strobe lights ranging from average power to high intensity, light meters, and film can mean an investment of $100,000. This, naturally, motivates the cinematographer to take excellent care of his equipment, which includes searching for leaks and cleaning after each use, particularly if he has been filming in salt water.

"Of course you must have mastered the basic elements of cinematography topside so you can take those skills underwater with you, and you *must* be a comfortable diver," emphasizes

The beauty of coral reefs, sea fans, and wildlife is captured in full color ▶ and movement with cinematography equipment that can cost up to $100,000. JACK MCKENNEY

McKenney. "You can't be worried about what's happening to you underwater and be creative at the same time. Diving has to become second nature to you."

Then, of course, there's the wildlife to contend with. Working with animals in the wild, you cannot always predict what will happen. Sometimes they may cooperate, sometimes they may not. And sometimes the cinematographer has to goad them into the desired behavior.

"If the scene calls for a lot of shark movement, and the sharks aren't cooperating, you may have to reach out and agitate them to get the desired effect. Of course you can always get shark handlers for that kind of thing," says McKenney.

Although McKenney trained "the hard way," first becoming a scuba instructor and doing films on the side, learning as he progressed, he would recommend a "more intelligent way to go about it" to anyone wishing to break into the industry.

After becoming a certified diver, he says, "I'd go to a really good film school like USC (University of Southern California), UCLA (University of California, Los Angeles), or the Brooks School of Photography (Santa Barbara). Then if I were going to work strictly as a cameraman, I'd try to get work in Hollywood in production. That means starting at the bottom as a camera loader, then progressing to camera assistant, and then camera operator. The next step up is director of photography, and that means you can get into the union. It's a very closed club and difficult to break into."

Like many other businesses, especially in Hollywood, the road to success is paved with the right contacts. Generally speaking, if a cinematographer works for someone once and does a good job—proves his dependability in meeting deadlines and quality of work—he will be hired again or referred to others for work. The road of the independent calls for a lot of self-motivation and a good business sense.

◄ Jack McKenney and his son John try to gain the cooperation of a film subject off Shark Reef in the Bahamas. BOB ABRAMS

The most important quality for an underwater cinematographer, however, is "being in love with your work," says McKenney. "When you're anywhere the diving is good, you can be down two hundred feet, and you look way, way up at this magical blue, with the fish coming in and out. It's really a great, great experience. I couldn't imagine doing anything else."

6

~~~~~~

THE RETAIL INDUSTRY

Dive shops are not usually inconspicuous.

As one drives along the road, a large red square bisected on the diagonal by a white slash—the traditional diver down symbol —looms as a beacon. Sometimes it is just an enormous flag flapping in the breeze. Sometimes the whole side of the building is painted red and white. However it is decorated, the dive shop attracts attention and beckons people to come learn about diving, about equipment, about the special camaraderie among those who venture beneath the surface of the water and become part of a different world.

The retail industry is the traditionally recognized business side of scuba diving. It is the nuts and bolts of a sport that is unique in the sense that, unlike jogging, tennis, or soccer, those who dive must depend totally on good quality equipment for their very lives. Since this makes scuba diving an equipment-intensive industry, it is little surprise that a large percentage of a diver's training involves learning how to select and operate equipment properly. And that equipment must be purchased at a dive shop.

But operating a dive shop is more than just running a store. The dive shop is usually a person's first encounter with divers and scuba diving. It is a place that educates the public about the spectacular beauty to be found underwater. It is where people find they can grasp adventure with both hands by signing up for a diving course or, if they are already certified, they can sign on for a score of dive trips. It is a place offering service and sociability, equipment and excitement. It is an escape—a link to the unknown.

From the Florida Keys to the Canadian border, from California to Australia's Great Barrier Reef, and from Japan to the azure waters of the South Pacific, dive shops attempt to meet the needs of their particular clientele.

The country's oldest known shop, San Diego Diver's Supply, in San Diego, California, deals with customers who consider it part of the community. Offering trips and social events, the shop has equipment from just about every manufacturer. Customers are generally local residents and college students, and sales of equipment and in-house events make it a hangout for those interested in the sport.

This differs from the tourist-oriented Central Pacific Divers on Maui, Hawaii, or even from the retail organization of Ray Lang, national spearfishing champion, who owns and operates three of the more successful shops in the country, including Diver's Den in Ft. Lauderdale, Florida, and Diver's Den South in Miami.

Lang's formula for success is two-fold. On one hand, he offers instruction to divers of all levels, from beginner to instructor, with numerous specialties—such as photography, wreck diver, cave diver, and deep diver—and a vast selection of equipment. On the other hand, he schedules trips, operates a boutique of active wear and bathing suits for nondivers, and plans picnics several times a year just for socializing.

"I think a lot of people get into diving to meet other people,"

Tony Zimos of the National Association of Skin Diving Schools points out the merits of a buoyancy-compensator vest to a customer visiting San Diego Diver's Supply—thought to be the oldest dive shop in the country. DENISE LANG

says Lang. "Picnics and softball games give customers a chance to get together and socialize, and nondiving members of the family feel included."

Part of operating a successful retail business is to know who your customers are going to be—whether you are primarily going to serve residents or tourists. Diver's Den South differs from Lang's recently opened Key Largo store, in that those patronizing the store in the Keys are primarily interested in renting equipment for dive trips instead of purchasing it. But they spend large amounts of money on impulse items such as sunglasses, T-shirts, resort wear, and suntan lotion.

Lakeland Divers, located in East Hanover, New Jersey, deals with divers looking for a different type of adventure—wreck diving in the cold waters off the New York and New Jersey coastline. Managed by David Sutton, marine researcher and author of a guide to wreck diving, Lakeland does a substantial business in dive trips, instruction, and the sale of equipment, including full wet suits, which are not needed in warmer, tropical waters.

"The retail diving business provides a good fixed income so you can continue to indulge your other diving interests and avocations," says Sutton. "Based on six days a week, year-round, a really good dive shop can provide an income of anywhere from $30,000 to $50,000 per year. Even a figure of $1 million per year is not out of the question, depending upon the shop's overall organization and location."

If the idea of opening or buying a dive shop sounds appealing and the money sounds good, how does one go about getting into the business?

The major trade and certification associations are a good place to begin. The growth of the scuba-diving industry was hampered for a long time by the fact that it is a nonspectator sport. No one sits on the side of a boat cheering as a diver takes a plunge to thirty-five feet in pursuit of a barracuda. As equipment technology has developed to the point where even young teenagers can participate with a reasonable degree of safety, the stumbling block of family members feeling left out has gradually been evaporating. This plus the attraction of an exotic experience has helped contribute to the sport's surge in popularity among all age groups. Because of the growing need for informed and well-trained personnel, major trade organizations have designed specific courses of study, recognizing the retail industry as a definable career choice.

Both the Professional Association of Diving Instructors and the National Association of Scuba Diving Schools sponsor detailed programs aimed at the successful operation of dive shops, which include such skills as equipment repair, equipment sales, telemarketing, scheduling recreational trips and social functions, preparation of newsletters, and personnel training.

Students at PADI International College actually set up a retail operation, complete with equipment displays and a newsletter. Practical retail and marketing techniques are also taught at

NASDS, which provides personal retail counseling to its affiliates anywhere in the world.

In addition to the major trade associations, a few independent services are available to the dive-shop owner. Hal Watts, holder of the *Guinness Book of World Records'* deep dive record, to 380 feet in 1967, has been a dive-shop owner, manufacturer's representative, and president of the Florida State Skin Diving Schools. He currently travels around the country conducting two-day progressive sales seminars to assist the retailer in upgrading his shop image, sales process, and salespeople.

"The diving industry is so connected with the economy," says Watts. "When money is tight, it's the last thing people try and the first thing they give up. We have been experiencing tremendous growth as a sport and an industry, and our biggest weakness right now is the lack of well-trained salespeople."

All who are involved in the diving industry, however, focus on service as the retailer's primary responsibility. That responsibility always carries with it the thought that a retailer's actions could save a life—or cost one.

"Stores are in business to instruct and sell equipment," says Ed Salamone of NASDS, "but there's a morality associated with it. That sounds a little heavy for a retail operation, but it is something we don't forget." The moral responsibility of maintaining ethical practices, a good servicing program, and a clean shop is taken seriously by the national trade associations, which keep close tabs on their affiliates through continued communication and feedback from manufacturers' representatives.

While the dive shop is the most obvious center of retail opportunities in the diving industry, jobs can also be found in representing equipment manufacturers around the country. The individual representing a manufacturer's line of diving equipment may either be considered a factory rep or an independent rep.

The factory rep is an employee of the equipment manufacturer, and it is his or her job to sell that line of equipment to dive shops, usually within a designated territory. Factory reps must be completely familiar with the manufacturer's operating procedures and line of equipment and be prepared to repair, as well as sell, a variety of items.

The independent rep works for a number of manufacturers, on a commission basis, and services a number of dive shops in a given territory. The independent could find himself dealing in equipment produced by Scubapro, Blue Water, US Divers, Fathom, ProSub, Dacor, Seaquest, and SeaTec, among others, rather than just one company's line.

With dive technology changing almost daily, equipment trade shows are a must for anyone considering entering the diving industry through retailing. The largest such trade show in the world is staged annually by the Diving Equipment Manufacturer's Association (DEMA) at sites announced in the trade journals.

Robert Grey, executive director of DEMA, says his organization has also taken an active role in establishing national standards for equipment. This is an important point in an industry that prides itself on self-regulation.

So if combining diving pleasure with salesmanship and a regular income sounds appealing, the retail industry provides plenty of opportunities for success both above the sea and below it. Anyone interested in getting into the retail business of diving should contact the trade associations listed at the end of this book, DEMA, or visit a local dive shop.

7

COMMERCIAL AIR DIVER

Sometimes they call themselves the hard-hat divers. They toss out comments like "Diving is an elevator—just a way to get to the job." And their diving conditions rarely include warm, caressing waters and exciting coral reefs. Rather they are described variously as "diving in a toilet," or "so cold and black, the only way you can function is automatically."

These divers are some of the most highly trained and toughened professionals in the industry. They are the commercial divers.

When an oil rig is being constructed, operated, and maintained out in the Gulf of Mexico or the treacherous waves of the frigid North Sea, commercial divers are the workhorses. They are the corporation's link between their financial investment and their product—oil. When a bridge or other submerged structure is suffering from corrosion or structural defects, a commercial diver performs the inspection, proposes a plan of action, and makes repairs. When cables need to be laid or terrain surveyed for construction, when hulls of two-thousand-ton vessels need to be repaired or parts of a ship salvaged, the commercial diver is the person to call.

The real heart of commercial diving is the transference and application of mechanical and electrical engineering as well as construction skills to an underwater setting. That means performance of those skills in an environment that is typically very stressful to the body.

A commercial diver must be able to adjust to being separated from family and cooped up in close quarters with strangers. The diving environment is sometimes hostile and usually cold. Visibility is nearly nonexistent. The hours are long over short periods of time, and the paycheck is dependent upon the jobs contracted.

So why would anyone become a commercial diver? Two reasons: the excitement and the money.

Commercial diving is a fantastic opportunity for the adventurous soul who has few responsibilities and who responds well to being called to a site anywhere in the world on short notice. Sometimes referred to as the gypsy of the diving industry, the commercial diver is responsible for the construction of all the world's offshore nuclear power plants and the underwater sources of the world's oil. He is on the spot where things are happening. And the monetary rewards are among the highest in the industry.

While newly graduated divers may start out at $15,000 to $17,000 per year, based on six to eight months of employment, those with relatively little experience, diving in the Gulf of Mexico for major corporations, can make $32,000 to $36,000 during a similar time period. Depending upon the project and location,

A commercial air diver has to transfer welding, repair, and construction ▶ skills to an underwater environment. GARY PARSONS / PROFESSIONAL DIVING SCHOOL OF NEW YORK

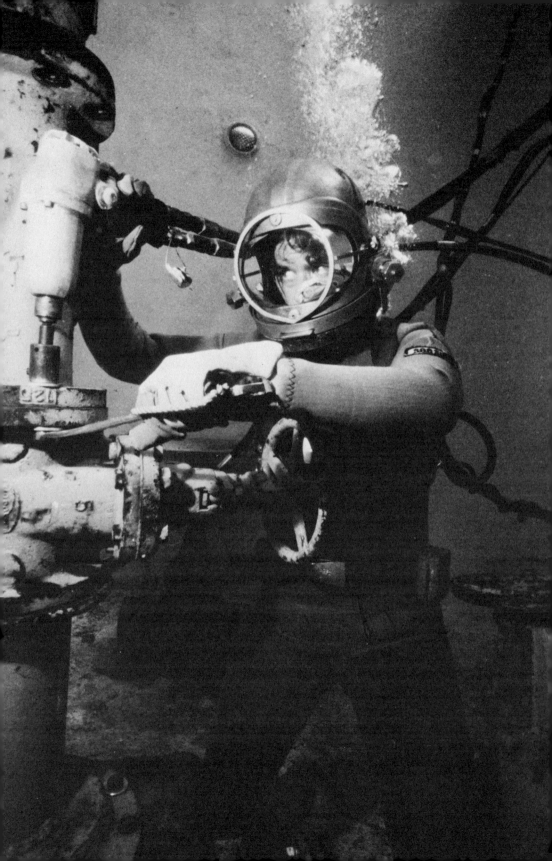

salaries for those more experienced can go as high as $75,000 to $100,000 for an eight-month work year.

The category of commercial diving also includes bell saturation diving, salvage diving, and technicians for remotely operated vehicles. The commercial air diver, however, is the backbone of the field. Put simply, the commercial air diver is one who performs his underwater tasks either with scuba gear on his back or with a full face mask connected to an air supply atop the ship or oil platform.

The area in which commercial air divers achieve a very high profile is in the oil industry. As early as 1900, drilling for oil was being performed from wharves extending out into the ocean from the shoreline or from wooden platforms constructed in shallow bays in marshes and bayous. When offshore operations of the petroleum industry grew as extensions of on-shore drilling, a new type of worker was needed to build, inspect, and maintain the oil rigs, which represent a major financial investment by the large oil companies. And every move further out to sea brought new problems to confront and conquer.

The world's thirst for oil, coupled with technological advancement, has established offshore commercial diving as an industry that may fluctuate with world economics but is not likely to diminish in stature.

Offshore oil work is the glamorous side of commercial diving. Much more common is inshore diving, which involves the construction and repair of everything from bridges to boats to buildings. This so-called harbor diving is sometimes regarded as the most difficult.

"When you're doing deep diving, you can usually see what you're working on because the water is clear at those depths," says Bill Smith, who, with Glenn Butler, founded the Professional Diving School of New York (PDSNY), a division of International Underwater Contractors. "Harbor diving is like diving in a toilet . . . you can't see because there's so much pollution. All you can do is feel."

Two important aspects of both harbor and offshore commercial work are inspection and photography. Whether the diver is working on an offshore oil rig or an inshore government or corporate construction project, a significant number of possible problems can be arrested by thorough and regular underwater inspections. Another purpose of inspections is to provide credible assurance to the operators, various government certifying or insurance agencies, and the public that all reasonable precautions have been taken to ensure the safety of the structure. Underwater photography is used as a tool to document the structure and visual inspection.

Underwater construction work also requires that commercial air divers use welding and burning skills. Just as their topside counterparts use welding torches for both original construction as well as repair work, so the commercial diver must apply this skill to projects ranging from pipelines and bridges to platforms and salvage.

The ability to get along well with diverse groups of people is one of the primary characteristics of the successful commercial air diver. Often, particularly in offshore oil work, the divers are isolated from the mainland for months at a time and must depend on their own inner resources and affability to help time pass when they are not working.

Les Joiner, admissions director for The Ocean Corporation (TOC), based in Houston, Texas, and a pioneer in nuclear power plant diving, says that bonds tend to form between commercial divers that are similar to those between police officers. "When you go into the water and put your life in someone else's hands, that makes for more than just your typical coworker kind of relationship. You have to have complete faith and trust in that person's abilities and reactions."

Joiner and Gary Parsons, training director for the Professional Diving School of New York, agree that the ideal candidate for commercial diving is a man in good health in his twenties with some experience either in construction or photography. It would be helpful if he had a scuba certification, but it is not necessary that he already know how to dive. Health requirements dictate that he not have heart, lung, or back problems, and he must have a similar psychological profile to that of an airline pilot. He cannot have claustrophobia and must have the ability to handle both physical and emotional stress.

Because offshore oil work is performed over many months in isolated locations and sometimes under spartan living conditions affording little privacy, women are not plentiful in the commercial diving field. This situation, of course, may change.

There are just a few women who have mastered the various specialties, such as underwater welding, photography, and inspection. The type of woman who would consider working in construction might consider commercial air diving. One area of the commercial industry that is providing exciting opportunities for women is the remotely operated vehicle technician. However, that will be dealt with separately in chapter 9.

Training as a commercial air diver can be obtained at a number of schools specifically geared to this demanding profession. Some schools have more extensive training facilities than others, and some have accreditations that others lack. Careful study should be given to the school's objectives and student training, as preparation in realistic working conditions is essential if the commercial diver is to perform his tasks proficiently and safely.

Whether a prospective student lives on the East Coast or West, there are reputable commercial schools available. From Divers Institute of Technology in Seattle, Washington, to the College of Oceaneering in Wilmington, California, to The Ocean Corporation in Houston, Divers Academy in Camden, New Jersey, Commercial Diving Institute in Whitestone, New York, and the Professional Diving School of New York in the Bronx, training programs are available year-round. Depending on the type of rating a student is looking for, courses of study last anywhere from four to eight months. Most schools provide a placement service for their graduates with commercial diving companies or at projects already underway.

Classes prepare the student in skills including underwater cutting and welding, inspection and photography, cable and pipe laying, diving physiology, emergency procedures, power mechanics, and seamanship. The seamanship course includes careful study of decompression and diving tables that chart how long a diver may remain at a specific depth or how soon he can return to that depth before his body absorbs a dangerous amount of nitrogen.

A new course of study sponsored by TOC attempts to give sport scuba divers who are performing commercial jobs the training they need to perform those tasks safely. Entitled The Commercial Scuba Diver, the eighty-hour course, which is crammed into eight days, recognizes that there are divers engaged in light commercial work who lack the proper equipment and skills.

Another unique form of training is offered by the College of Oceaneering in California. Students there can receive an Associate in Applied Science degree. Courses are aimed at benefiting the student academically while providing commercial skills necessary for employment.

Bill Smith of PDSNY feels the quality of commercial divers has improved because of the rigorous training now provided by the commercial diving schools. But, as in most professions, the newly graduated diver must start at the bottom—both literally and figuratively.

"For the first couple of months on an oil project, you chip paint and change valves. This gives the new diver time to acclimate to the unique working atmosphere on an oil rig," says Smith. "Then he goes on to be a panel operator, watching and learning the dive tables. Once he's ready, and that is determined by the supervisor, he becomes what's called a tender."

Tenders monitor other divers' breathing rates and the mixtures of breathable gases used on deeper dives. They may be called upon to retrieve a diver in distress. Once this period of competency building is reached, then and only then does he attain diver status.

Full-fledged divers may then be promoted to supervisory posi-

Tenders assist commercial air divers entering the water by keeping air hoses free of tangles. GARY PARSONS / PROFESSIONAL DIVING SCHOOL OF NEW YORK

tions. They are first charged with the responsibility for other divers and then, finally, with an entire project.

"All the while, the diver is building his confidence, his skills, and his relationships with others on the project," says Smith. Whether the commercial air diver goes to work off the frigid coast of Iceland, the balmy Gulf of Mexico, or the many inshore sites requiring the services of highly trained underwater technicians, the hierarchy of advancing in the business is the same. But the actual job rarely is.

A listing of schools offering training in commercial diving can be found on pages 124–125.

8

<hr>

BELL SATURATION
DIVER

You have probably seen pictures of underwater habitats in magazines—those colossal structures on the bottom of the ocean from which scientific divers swim each day to perform experiments and to which they return for rest. Or perhaps you have been seduced by the adventure and mystery of living under water through characters like Captain Nemo in the classic *Twenty Thousand Leagues Under the Sea.*

But bell saturation diving flooded into America's living rooms and general consciousness via the television set in 1984. The catalyst was a curious explorer and filmmaker, Peter Gimbel, who allowed the public inside his diving bell as he tried to uncover the secrets of the sunken Italian ocean liner, the *Andrea Doria.*

It was a mystery that began in the fog on July 25, 1956, at 11:09 P.M. when the Swedish vessel *Stockholm* rammed the nearly seven-hundred-foot-long floating palace. Within eleven hours, despite new technologies in shipbuilding, including twelve airtight compartments, the *Andrea Doria* slipped beneath the surface of the Atlantic, fifty miles off the coast of Nantucket Island, to rest on the sand 235 feet below.

Her sinking took the lives of fifty people and personal property, original art treasures and industrial goods valued in millions of dollars. The *Andrea Doria* not only boasted several banks, three movie theaters, and elegant shops, but a lounge that sported the masterpieces of Michelangelo, Cellini, Raphael, and Titian.

Gimbel's first dive on the ship took place on the day following the sinking. His mission was to take photos for *Life* magazine. Over the ensuing twenty years he made numerous other dives, drawn not only by the tales of grandeur, but also by the question as to why the luxury liner sank so quickly. Finally, in 1981, after much preparation, he and an assembled crew dove the treacherous currents surrounding the *Doria* in the hopes of getting some answers.

Because of the depth of the ship and the hours needed for securing cables, equipment, and actual diving time, the most efficient method of working on the *Andrea Doria* was bell saturation diving. The viewing public was allowed inside the cylindrical iron diving bell on a television special. What they saw were cramped quarters and tired divers. They heard crew members talk like Alvin the Chipmunk—a byproduct of the mixture of helium and oxygen used in the bell.

While the adventure on the *Andrea Doria* brought saturation diving into the public's vocabulary, the more common use of saturation, or SAT, diving—as it is commonly referred to—is in a commercial enterprise or research forum.

First, what exactly is SAT diving?

When the body is subjected to increased pressure, such as in deep diving, increased amounts of gas will filter into the blood system and tissues. Nitrogen, the principal inert gas (a gas the body cannot use) and the gas that makes up nearly 80 percent of our air, is the primary offender. The deeper a diver goes, the more nitrogen will be absorbed by his body until it is saturated.

The process reverses when the diver comes back up to the surface. The body is able to gradually throw off the nitrogren— or decompress—unless the diver comes up too quickly. If this occurs, he can get the bends as the nitrogen, which has not had time to dissolve, bubbles up in his blood and tissues. The bends can cause death.

The process of saturation and decompression takes time. For commercial operations, which may be performed at depths ranging from two hundred to five hundred feet, the system of saturation and decompression can take from two days to two weeks in order to ensure the safety of the divers. As you can see, if this were to be done on a daily basis, there would be very little work done underwater because most of the time would be taken up in saturation and decompression.

The U.S. Navy experimented with saturation diving in the late 1950s and early 1960s. The first saturation habitat, built off the coast of France in 1962, is credited to Captain Jacques-Yves Cousteau.

Under SAT conditions, the diver (or team of divers) works out of a habitat whose atmosphere is maintained at approximately the same pressure as that of the surrounding water or working depth. This habitat can be one of several types. An ocean-floor installation is generally large and remains fixed to the bottom. Divers live and work there, using the installation as home for the time they are underwater. The simple diving bell is actually a bell-shaped chamber that can hold two to ten divers. And there is also a habitat which is a pressurized chamber fastened to the deck of the ship from which the diver travels to his working depth each day in a pressurized capsule.

The habitat most commonly used in commercial installations, however, is called a lock-out submersible. Shaped like a large metal sausage, it is designed with at least two separate compartments that allow the divers to enter and exit the water while the habitat is submerged. The air breathed in the SAT submersible is often a mixture of helium and oxygen. Pure oxygen causes poi-

A diving bell owned by International Underwater Contractors (IUC), prior to launching. Bells such as this can support diving services to three-hundred-foot depths. GARY PARSONS / PROFESSIONAL DIVING SCHOOL OF NEW YORK

soning at great depths. Although the helium-oxygen mixture has proven to be most efficient, the side effect is that the divers sound like Alvin the Chipmunk when they speak. This is the same effect that is achieved if you take a breath of helium from a balloon and then speak.

The refinement of SAT diving conditions has been a boon to the oil industry. As offshore oil operations move into greater water depths and more hostile environments, all costs increase rapidly. Exploratory drilling is done from mobile rigs, while many operating wells are drilled from fixed platforms, complete with production and maintenance facilities. Because of the tremendous costs associated with oil production, SAT diving has proven to be the most efficient.

According to Bill Smith of PDSNY, the value to large companies of saturation diving is that "teams of divers can work around the clock for up to twenty-eight days at a time. Each team will work eight- or twelve-hour shifts, all at the same pressure, with work going on continuously."

In addition, the value of SAT diving to the researcher is that he or she can observe the ocean's wildlife over a period of days, uninterrupted by the descents, ascents, and limited bottom time restricting an accurate observation of animal behavior.

Actual work conditions vary as greatly for the SAT diver as those for the commercial air diver. Laying cables, welding, visual inspection, photography, and general construction work must all take place in a cold, often black, wet environment. Given the

IUC's Mermaid II is a two-person submersible, capable of working at a depth of one thousand feet. GARY PARSONS / PROFESSIONAL DIVING SCHOOL OF NEW YORK

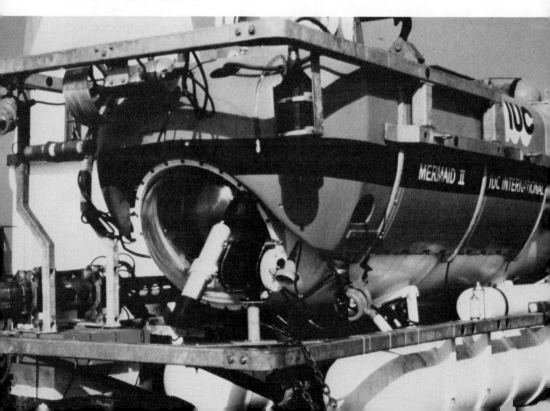

IUC's Beaver MK IV submersible going to work in an Egyptian oil field. Five-person crews can work out of the Beaver to depths of two thousand feet.   GARY PARSONS / PROFESSIONAL DIVING SCHOOL OF NEW YORK

physical labor and the depths at which tasks must be performed, SAT diving is often exhausting work. The drawing card, again, in this field, is the salary, which is partly based on the diver's worth to the prospective employer. "The more tricks you do, the more valuable you are," says Les Joiner of The Ocean Corporation, "and of course, that also translates into dollars and cents."

Despite the high salary range ($40,000 to $100,000), whether working for oil or construction companies, research or government agencies, life in a diving habitat is not for everyone.

First, accommodations are cramped. Jack McKenney, who served as head photographer for Gimbel's *Doria* adventure, described the instruction process for living in a bell as "like being born all over again. We even had to learn how to flush a toilet properly."

Not only is recreation space limited (recreational activity usually consists of reading, playing cards on one's bunk, and sleeping!), but so is eating room (the bells are equipped with food warmers) and dressing room. After all, the purpose of being down there is to suit up and go to work, and commercial suits are very bulky!

Those who find it difficult to be cooped up in an automobile with the same people for a ride across country may find it difficult to live under the stressful conditions in a diving bell. A SAT diver must live with two to five other people, lacking any privacy for up to a month in a space that is sometimes smaller than a one-car garage.

Another thing the bell SAT diver must become accustomed to is his total dependence on the surface. Food, water, temperature control, and communication come from the surface. Someone who suffers from claustrophobia or needs to feel in complete charge will not be happy or successful as a SAT diver.

The health of divers living in such a closed environment is of prime importance. Therefore, health requirements for the prospective SAT diver are stringent. Generally, those who are prone to asthma, ear infections, sinus infections, severe skin disorders, physical disabilities, or mental illness would not be allowed into a SAT diving program.

There is also the candidate's personality profile, which school admissions directors say must be assessed during training. Like the commercial air diver, "stranded" for weeks in close quarters with the same faces, under physically and emotionally stressful conditions, the SAT diver's life depends on his fellow divers and technicians. Behavior must be congenial and professional, and the SAT diver must inspire trust.

Because the diving bell is a dependent vessel, there is a need also for life-support technicians in addition to the actual working divers. The technician is responsible for the complicated life-giving gas mixtures and the monitoring equipment needed to keep track of those gases in the diving bell. Sometimes the life-support technician is also trained as a diver medic. This career will be discussed in chapter 12.

Training in SAT diving is obtained exclusively through commercial diving schools. Two specialties of SAT diving include bounce-bell diving and North Sea bell diving. Bounce-bell diving is often considered the most stressful type of saturation diving. This involves moving—or "bouncing"—the diving bell from one pressure level to another to get several different jobs done. North Sea bell diving is a highly specialized form of saturation diving because of the severity of working conditions in the treacherous and undependable waters of the North Sea. Certification of North Sea bell divers comes under the jurisdiction of the United Kingdom Department of Energy.

Although specific facilities and courses may vary slightly from school to school, generally the prospective SAT diver will be trained in courses ranging from living under pressure, shore support logistics, and mixed gas analysis to bell emergency procedures and diving systems design. Also of great importance to the prospective diver is decompression theory and operations, tethered diving operations, and underwater welding and cutting. As of this writing, the Professional Diving School of New York is the only commercial diving school in the United States accredited to certify those who wish to work as North Sea bell divers.

Owing to the relatively small number of commercial divers and the fact that all forms of commercial diving, particularly saturation diving, involve complicated technologies and equipment, commercial diving schools are not as plentiful as sport diving schools. Training is obtainable in most parts of the country, however, as school sites range from New York, New Jersey, and Texas to California and Washington. Because of the very stringent requirements placed upon bell saturation divers by both corporations and governments, it is important that anyone wishing to enter this challenging field carefully check out the various schools available for thoroughness of training and preparation.

Thanks to the professional career orientation of commercial operations, financial aid may be obtained for most courses of study.

9

ROV TECHNICIAN

The morning of January 28, 1986, dawned on millions of enthusiastic space fans from all over the world jamming the beaches and parks around Cape Canaveral, Florida. Despite the unseasonable 24-degree temperature of the previous night, all systems were go for the nation's fifty-sixth space launch. The shuttle *Challenger,* which had suffered three delays, to the impatience and disappointment of a country used to clockwork lift-offs, was finally going to take off. The $1.2 billion *Challenger* would be ushering in a new era in space exploration that day as it carried the first civilian astronaut. Christa McAuliffe, a high school social studies teacher from Concord, New Hampshire. She joined astronauts Francis Scobee, Ellison Onizuka, Michael Smith, Gregory Jarvis, Judith Resnik, and Ronald McNair. But the history-making flight was to make the history books in a tragic way.

Just seventy-two seconds into the flight, as millions cheered, cried, and sang "God Bless America" below, the shuttle's orbiter yawed to the right, and the rocket booster broke loose and pivoted into the fuel tank. The explosion that ensued plunged the astronauts' compartment fifty-five thousand feet into the Atlantic.

Although small pieces of debris from the *Challenger* were found floating fifteen miles offshore, the largest pieces—and the primary source of answers to why the shuttle blew up—lay scattered across forty miles underwater at depths from one hundred to nearly two thousand feet. While navy divers set about recovery immediately, the National Aeronautics and Space Administration (NASA) put out a call for deep-water assistance. Within days, a flotilla of underwater robots equipped with side-scan radar, video cameras, pincerlike arms, high-speed still cameras, and sophisticated communication abilities was scouring the ocean floor. Supplied by the navy, the Harbor Branch Foundation in Ft. Pierce, Florida, and a private company in California, remotely operated vehicles (ROVs) became as well known to the grieving public as their automobiles. The Johnson-Sea-Link II, Deep Drone, Cord, Orion, and Gemini carried scientists, NASA officials, and engineers to depths of fifteen hundred feet to identify and photograph *Challenger*'s wreckage. They returned to the surface vessels with the shuttle's four flight recorders, pieces of solid rocket boosters, the plastic package containing materials that McAuliffe had planned to use to teach schoolchildren lessons from space, and, finally, the astronauts' compartment. Recovery of the shuttle, and indeed the astronauts' remains, would have been impossible without the ROVs.

While scuba and traditional commercial diving enjoy a history of technological development stretching back to Homer's *Iliad,* the history of remotely operated vehicles, Atmospheric Diving

Wreckage from the space shuttle *Challenger,* retrieved from the Atlan- ▶ tic Ocean, is lifted on board the deck of the U.S. Coast Guard Cutter *Dallas.* NASA

The Johnson-Sea-Link I was called in by NASA to search for pieces of the ill-fated space shuttle *Challenger.* A four-person submersible, it could identify and photograph sections deeper than twenty-six hundred feet. HARBOR BRANCH FOUNDATION

Systems (ADS), and deep Rovers is in the making. And with technology introducing new elements every six months or so, underwater robotics is one of the most exciting areas of the diving industry today.

Although the traditional commercial diving operation remains the most often used method of completing underwater tasks, manned and remotely operated vehicles are rapidly becoming the primary means of performing many complicated undersea tasks and inspection missions both offshore and at inland water sites.

Standard commercial diving operations are limited to about a one-thousand-foot working depth. However, the oil industry's search for new offshore resources has stretched those depths to

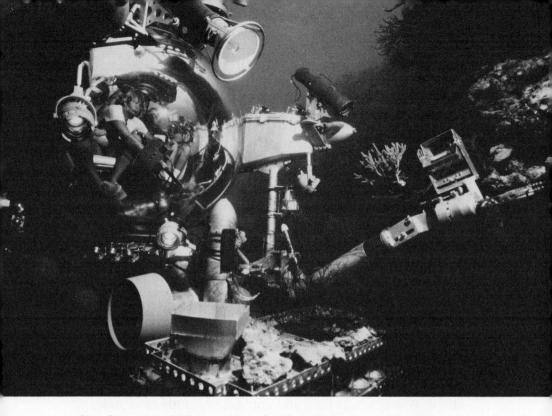

The Johnson-Sea-Link II, equipped with high-resolution television cameras, side-scan sonar, and manipulator arms capable of lifting 150 pounds, carried scientists and NASA officials down to the various *Challenger* wreckage sites. HARBOR BRANCH FOUNDATION

more than eight thousand feet. And researchers, as well as the military, are heading into deeper waters daily. The assistance of vehicles capable of performing at those increased depths assures productivity and progress in a variety of areas.

A ROV is exactly what its name implies—an undersea vehicle remotely operated from a ship or surface command center through a tether or acoustic link, which allows for control of the vehicle and data exchange. ROVs come in many sizes and complexities, from the simple "remote eyeball" used to serve as the operator's visual porthole beneath the surface to the ROV that can perform difficult mechanical repairs while videotaping the entire process.

ROVs all have their own means of propulsion but are connected to the ship or command center which supplies the electricity. People who operate ROVs are called pilots, and the operation of a vehicle is "flying." A view of the command center shows an elaborate system of controls and display monitors through which the pilot can direct the ROV's movements and see what the ROV is "seeing."

The increasing costs of putting manned submersibles into the sea with all their attendant support systems has contributed to the growing popularity and use of ROVs. Gone are the human needs for food, water, warmth, and health care. Gone are the psychological stresses of SAT diving. Gone, too, is the concern over possible loss of life while performing tasks in hazardous conditions. The machine performs while the pilot sits in relative comfort. There are no restrictions on depth and continuous performance. The ROV's work shift is limited only by the pilot's fatigue.

Recovery of the space shuttle *Challenger* is but one aspect of the ROV's practical uses and applications. Others include:

inspection and maintenance   locating and checking the condition of deeply submerged structures and performing simple maintenance tasks

monitoring   observing and measuring commercial and scientific projects as they progress

exploration drilling support   observing commercial oil wellhead drilling systems and the operation and changing of valves

survey work   measuring and sampling the physical features of the ocean bottom

diver assistance   supporting diver activities

search and identification   locating and identifying objects on the sea floor

installation and retrieval   assisting with the installation of fixed structures and the retrieval of objects

cleaning   removing barnacles and debris (particularly important on expensive oil rig installations)

At the time of this writing, the only school providing training on ROVs is the Underwater Vehicle Training Center (UVTC) based in Houston, Texas. Headed by Eric Galerne, UVTC is a branch of International Underwater Contractors, Inc., the largest privately owned company providing underwater services worldwide. Because of this connection, graduates of UVTC's eight-week program not only obtain the latest in technological training, but assistance in securing a job.

While women are scarce throughout the rest of the commercial diving industry because of adverse conditions and lack of privacy on long-term work platforms, piloting ROVs provides an excellent point of entry for them, as they can easily perform short-term projects and inshore work.

Randy Hanks, training director for UVTC, says they can take anyone who has never been around the water and train him to pilot a ROV, "but the best ROV pilots are divers—people who have been there, done it, and know what they're looking at on the screen."

Any high school graduate who is eighteen or older can apply. Individuals with a strong mechanical aptitude and / or experience in general hydraulic electrical / electronic systems, robotics, and related technologies are prime candidates. And former military personnel with aircraft, navigation, or weapons-systems electronic ratings generally excel in the industry.

Despite its sounding like the "cleanest" of commercial diving careers, ROV piloting faces its own set of unique challenges to one's safety, Hanks stresses. "For one thing, you are always taught to keep electricity away from water, but there you are on a ship with electrical cables everywhere, water sloshing all over, operating an electrical unit," he says. Operating in kelp beds is difficult, and attacks by sharks on cable lines must be dealt with. The ROV pilot must be able to recognize sonar interference from schools of fish, and pollution and silt present visual problems. "And then there's the cold—electronics is affected by temperature."

But the increased demand for ROV pilots and technicians—those who repair ROVs and assist the pilots—makes this specialty one of the fastest growing in the field. Pay scales reflect the need. Entry-level ROV technicians can earn from $110 to $150 per day, based on a twelve-hour day (whether you work twelve hours or not, says Hanks). Entry-level ROV pilots can command salaries of $165 to $215 per day, depending upon the company. Inshore work is paid on an "in-shop time" basis of $9 to $12 per hour.

Imagine this scenario: A component of an offshore oil rig has just broken down one thousand feet below the surface of the water. Each hour the operation is shut down costs thousands of dollars and causes hundreds of tension headaches. A SAT diving team is told to prepare for descent and repairs. They climb into the diving bell and begin the long process of compression.

But wait. . . . what is that on the corner of the ship? A man, dressed in jeans and T-shirt, jumps into what looks like a bulky space suit and leaps overboard. A few hours later, the repairs are complete and Superdiver is treating himself to a well-deserved meal while the SAT team is not even halfway into its pressurization.

Superdiver indeed! The Atmospheric Diving System, which was first developed by the British in 1969, looks like a bulky space suit. Nicknamed Jim, it is a one-person submersible capable of taking a human down to approximately three thousand feet almost as easily as swimming to the bottom of a swimming pool.

Termed a one-atmosphere diving system, the beauty of ADS is that it keeps the diver's pressure at sea level, supplying "regular" air at a comfortable temperature, despite the depth to which it is taken. Thus, this suit eliminates the need for elaborate and time-consuming compression and decompression procedures.

The Wasp and Mantis, descendents of Jim, were both designed by Graham Hawkes, English engineer and president and chief executive officer of Deep Ocean Engineering and Deep Ocean Technology. They have revolutionized work in the oil fields as well as the underwater research area. An improvement on the Jim design, both the Wasp and Mantis include the power of self-locomotion, controlled by foot pedals. This inspires the sensation of flying a helicopter underwater.

Manned submersibles of this sort have an advantage over ROVs because humans can make observations and split-second decisions and take action immediately as situations change.

Jim Joiner, president of the College of Oceaneering in Wilmington, California, attributes the growth of Atmospheric Diving Systems to the need to dive in ever-increasing depths "and the limitations of man's ability to undergo saturation for extended periods." Owned by Oceaneering International, the largest contractor of ADS worldwide, the College of Oceaneering offers the only training available (as of this writing), and that training is available only to selected divers.

Applicants must have completed related courses in commercial diving, finishing in the top half of their class, and be subjected to personal interviews. They may need to take additional courses. Those accepted for training on the ADS start first on Jim, where the main challenge is maneuverability. After Jim, they train on Wasp for approximately thirty hours.

Since the College of Oceaneering has recently been accredited as a junior college, a degree of Associate in Applied Science can be awarded for commercial diving courses of study.

Another Graham Hawkes design, and a descendent of Wasp and Mantis, is Deep Rover. The current Deep Rover is only a little over eight feet long, seven and one-half feet high, and six feet wide, with its hull pressure-tested to five thousand feet (it will collapse at twelve thousand). It resembles a helicopter, and one can wear street clothes as he "flies" it. Protruding from the hull are two manipulator arms which have the sensitivity to pick up a quarter and the strength to lift more than two hundred pounds.

Future versions will go even deeper. Deep Rover II, to be made of a glass sphere instead of acrylic, will be designed for excursions of down to twenty thousand feet, and Deep Rover III is being planned to withstand the pressures of more than thirty-five thousand feet.

The implications for commercial operations as well as research and recreation are enormous. Deep Rovers will be utilized by the government, the National Oceanic and Atmospheric Administration (NOAA), fish and wildlife associations, private industry, pharmacological research, environmental agencies—and the general public.

Dr. Sylvia Earle, marine scientist extraordinaire, pioneering aquanaut, author, lecturer, curator of the California Academy of Sciences, and cofounder and vice president of Deep Ocean Engineering and Deep Ocean Technology, views Deep Rover as the advent of an exciting era in undersea transportation.

"Why should there be any limits?" she demands. "The reasons don't apply anywhere else. People used to say it is impossible to go to Antarctica. We did it. Impossible to go to the moon. We

Piloted by pioneering aquanaut Sylvia Earle, Deep Rover is capable of depths exceeding five thousand feet. Designed by English inventor Graham Hawkes, future versions of Deep Rover could take the public on exciting sight-seeing trips to the ocean's floor.   DEEP OCEAN ENGINEERING

have done it. This is the beginning of the greatest exploration ever. . . . There's so much to discover underwater—mountain chains, for example."

And those discoveries will be available in the future as families board Deep Rovers for vacation excursions in much the same way as they board buses or planes now.

Each new area of robotics has its strengths and contributions to make to both industry and the individual. The bottom line is the flinging away of shackles to land as humans are able to plunge deeper and deeper into parts of Earth never before explored.

Science fiction will have to look for new horizons as cities under the sea become reality and the human race is unfettered by atmosphere and pressure. Ocean engineering is wide open to exploration and discovery, similar to the aviation industry of fifty years ago. Much is being done for the first time, and robotics is one way to get involved.

"You can sit on the crest of a mountain and look up and wish all you want," says Earle, "but you won't go anywhere unless you build wings."

Underwater robotics are the new wings of man.

10

SALVAGE DIVER

It was the kind of discovery that pulled at the adventurer from deep within each person's soul around the world.

After seventeen years of struggle, false hope, death, and enormous expenditures, Mel Fisher heard the sweet words he knew would come someday—"We found it! We found it! It's here!"

It was the remains of the Spanish galleon *Nuestra Señora de Atocha,* discovered off the coast of Key West in the form of fifteen-inch silver bars "stacked up like cordwood as far as the eye could see." In addition to the silver ingots, weighing in at seven tons, were the usual fantasy-come-true wooden treasure chests overflowing with gold coins and other valuables. Estimates for the total find hovered around $400 million.

The sixty-four-year-old Fisher, who nearly drowned at eleven years of age trying out a homemade diving helmet fashioned out of a paint can and bicycle tires, always maintained that the profit was secondary. "It was the hunt, the challenge," he told one interviewer.

He began in the salvage diving business by working on someone else's salvage project. It was then he caught the fever to look for the *Atocha,* sunk in a 1622 hurricane while en route to Spain, laden with treasure. After hours of research and poring over more than fifty thousand decaying documents from the 1600s, Fisher turned up the original seventeenth-century salvor's report that indicated the ship could be found near the desolate Marquesas Keys, off Key West.

Salvage diving has drawn dedicated participants from ancient times to the present. Pirates were salvors. Anyone wishing for that pot of gold at the bottom of the ocean tried his hand at salvaging. The very word *salvage*—defined by *Webster's Ninth New Collegiate Dictionary* as "the act of saving or rescuing a ship or its cargo" and "compensation paid for saving a ship or its cargo from the perils of the sea or for the lives and property rescued in a wreck"—appeals to the hero, the explorer lurking in our personalities.

Often described interchangeably with the term *wreck diving,* salvage diving is, in fact, a distinct entity, separated primarily by the word *compensation.* While wreck diving is an avocation done for sport (but perhaps with the hope of finding a Spanish doubloon or plate from an historic wreck), salvage diving is a business. Salvaging is methodical and often dangerous. It covers an area broader than the glamorous recovery of lost ships. The salvage diver is in the business with a pure economic return in mind.

That economic return *can* come from ancient lost ships, but more often it takes the form of recovered cargo from recently sunk vessels. Industrial recovery, the removal of hazards to man and the underwater environment, and the removal of chemicals and other elements and minerals accidentally sunk comprise the majority of a salvor's business.

The salvage of a ship, cargo, or equipment involves not only

The spine of a ship wrecked off the coast of the Bahamas is all that is left after time and salvage divers have stripped it bare. FLORIDA INSTI-TUTE OF TECHNOLOGY

the technical aspects of recovery but the legal ownership of those items recovered. In the case of Mel Fisher, the state of Florida originally claimed 25 percent of all treasure recovered back in the late 1970s. Fisher dutifully deposited the state's fair share, and then the federal government declared that it owned *all* of the treasure, present and future. Taking his case all the way to the Supreme Court, Fisher, in 1982, finally won the judgment that he is the sole owner of any treasure recovered. (As it turned out, the profit had to be split with crew members and more than eighty backers who helped finance his expeditions.)

A salvor who recovers a ship or craft, or its cargo, without prior agreement with the owner, must file a claim in the United States district court nearest to the port in which the salved items are landed.

Because of the nature of salvaging, there are as many techniques and types of equipment employed as there are reasons for diving. Each project is different and requires a different methodology, but the key word is *method*. It is not a haphazard business, and while diving schools do not teach salvaging per se, this type of diving requires the best of sport and commercial diving techniques and skills, as well as equipment. Training at a commercial dive school, including courses in search and recovery, photography, and diver medicine, would be helpful background to the aspiring salvor.

If an individual is going out for a minor salvage operation—that

The sunken steel barge *Coatwise I,* weighing nearly six hundred tons, is salvaged from seventy feet of water at the entrance channel to Norfolk, Virginia. GARY PARSONS / PROFESSIONAL DIVING SCHOOL OF NEW YORK

is, diving in relatively shallow water to look for anchors, instruments, or pottery—he can carry these items to the surface by hand. Another method of raising recovered articles from the ocean floor is through the use of flotation devices the diver can attach. If the article is heavy, as in the case of an anchor, a line might be attached and then the anchor lifted by turning a winch on board ship.

Often, sediment must be removed from the objects before they are lifted without causing too much disturbance to the surrounding sea floor. Also, water must be displaced or the object will weigh too much to lift. This requires additional equipment, including electronics needed at the salvage site.

One of the grander and most costly salvage projects captured the romantic interest and memory of the world in September 1985. It began with what has been termed the greatest maritime tragedy of all time.

On April 14, 1912, in the wee hours of the morning, the British steamer *Titanic* hit an iceberg. Within two and a half hours, the ship disappeared from sight, taking the lives of 1,522 people, including many wealthy Americans who wanted to make the historic maiden crossing on the world's largest "unsinkable" ship.

For decades, the *Titanic,* which sank off the coast of Newfoundland, approximately sixteen hundred miles northeast of New York City, was the object of speculation, stories, and research. It had never been found.

Robert Ballard, head of the Deep Submergence Laboratory at Woods Hole Oceanographic Institution in Woods Hole, Massachusetts, and leader of a joint mission of French and American scientists, made the first sighting at 1:40 A.M. on September 1. What he saw was a giant boiler on the ocean floor, surrounded by debris including luggage and cases of French wine. Then he saw the ship—all of it—at thirteen thousand feet!

Ballard's joint research / salvage expedition, financed primarily by the U.S. Navy's Office of Naval Research, boasted some of the most sophisticated and expensive equipment available today. High-resolution French-developed sonar assisted in methodically scanning a hundred-square-mile search area five hundred miles east of Newfoundland.

When a massive object became apparent, the team then employed a new computerized ROV, the Argo, sixteen feet in length and equipped with sonar, powerful strobe lights, and sophisticated video equipment. Capable of descending to twenty thousand feet, the Argo was able to transmit photos of the *Titanic* through cables connected to special towing cranes on the ship.

During the following year, thanks to the use of both manned submersibles and ROVs, Ballard presented the world with photographs of the *Titanic* and its cargo—scattered across hundreds of yards—12,500 feet below the North Atlantic. While he has proven it is possible to salvage artifacts from the majestic wreck, whether the *Titanic* will ever become the biggest salvage operation in history remains to be seen. Reinforcing his conviction that the *Titanic* should remain undisturbed, Ballard placed a commemorative plaque, donated by the Titanic Historical Society, on the vessel's stern during his seventh dive to the site in the submersible Alvin. Adventurers from Texas to London, however, announced plans to employ their own submersibles for recovery of artifacts in the near future.

Even if the *Titanic* were not sitting at such a great depth, the dangers of salvage diving and recovery must be considered. Those who dove on the *Andrea Doria* told of walls collapsing and the ship's crumbling at a touch. Salvage diving is often performed in water where there is little visibility. Extra safety precautions must be taken to prevent divers' being separated from one another or trapped in an unstable vessel, and to ensure their safe return to the ship.

Despite precautions, freak accidents can happen. In 1975, twenty-one-year-old Dirk Fisher, Mel Fisher's son, uncovered a bronze cannon that unquestionably belonged to the *Atocha,* although remnants of the ship were scattered over such a wide area that it took another decade to find the main pile. One week later, Dirk, his wife, Angel, and another diver, Rick Gage, died when their salvage boat capsized in a squall.

The dangers are present. But so is the profit. And as long as man harbors romance, adventure, and the desire for riches in his heart, so too will there be salvage divers.

11

MARINE BIOLOGIST / ECOLOGIST

Sitting before the television set, we watch the colorful fish floating before our eyes. Captain Jacques Cousteau directs our attention to the ocean floor, where a phenomenon of the sea is about to take place—the march of the spiny lobster. One by one the blackish blue crustaceans line up head-to-tail and begin their walk to deeper waters, where they will spawn their young before returning.

What a great job those divers have, we think, as we see them photographing and recording this moment in history. Marine biology is the place to be!

Anyone who has ever been mesmerized by a Jacques Cousteau television show, participated in a whale watch, seen porpoises leaping into the air at a public aquarium, or even studied freshwater fish in a home aquarium, has probably been tantalized by the fun and fascination of working with marine animals in the field of marine biology.

What most people think of as marine biology, however, represents a small facet of the overall picture. Marine biology—the study of the life cycle of marine animals—is difficult if not impossible to separate from marine ecology—how the study of particular animals fit into the total marine world. Today, the terms *marine biology* and *marine ecology* are often used interchangeably to describe the areas of study and actual projects in the undersea realm.

And thanks to the continued development of diving equipment and underwater photographic equipment, scuba diving is an integral tool of the research scientist. Marine biologists are able to use diving to help chart the distribution of plants and animals in both shallow and deep-water areas. They can conduct experiments to find out how marine organisms survive in saltwater or freshwater environments. They can study how fish breathe, move, and sense what is happening around them.

Much of the research of marine biologists is now directed toward the continued survival of our commercial fishes and making fishing more economical. Marine biologists also continue to search for new foods and drugs from the sea while trying to find better ways of raising underwater crops.

All of this can be accomplished underwater through the use of scuba gear and techniques. But first we need to get a clear understanding of how the biology and ecology of the ocean go hand in hand before we can appreciate the technical expertise and projects underway today.

Technically speaking, marine biology deals with the individual organism. It is the study of its growth rate, its reproductive system and behavior, and its life cycle in general.

Marine ecology is the study of what is on the rock next to that organism. What is the organism's relationship to the creature next to it, and how is the organism affected by that creature? What does the organism eat, and where does it fit into the overall scheme of life in the sea?

Since the two fields are so interrelated, is there a place for the individual who is interested only in studying shark behavior or the mating cycles of sea turtles?

Morgan Hardwick-Witman, marine biologist and coordinator of Northeastern University's program at the Marine Science and Maritime Studies Center at Nahant, Massachusetts, feels that the person who views marine biology as one-dimensional is limiting himself impossibly.

"I get a lot of students who come back from a whale watch and are all excited. They tell me they want to dedicate their lives to studying the humpback whale. I tell them, fine, but there's only so much you can do with them," says Hardwick-Witman. "The problem with a strict limitation like that is accessibility, for one. It's hard to get near a whale on a continuing basis. Secondly, behavioral studies are always influenced by the presence of the diver."

Dr. Bill Lindberg, assistant professor in the fisheries and aquaculture department at the University of Florida, has been a diving scientist for more than ten years. He agrees that there are some marine biologists who deal only with specific animals, but it is necessary to study how the animal moves in its environment.

"Marine biologists unfortunately gave the connotation 'Well, gee whiz, let's go underwater and see what we find,'" says Lindberg. "If you are a practicing research scientist and your colleagues view you as a 'Gee whiz' character, you will suffer professionally. Today's scientist must be able to see the total picture."

"Seeing the total picture" allows those who love the study of marine life and diving to combine all the elements into a fun career. But research is research, whether one is wearing a lab coat or scuba tanks. The point must be stressed that the marine biologist / ecologist is a scientist first.

"It is much easier to teach a scientist to dive than to teach a diver how to be a scientist," says Dr. Bert Kobayashi, marine biologist and head of the sport-diving program at the University of California, San Diego (UCSD). A certified research diver and

teacher of marine ecology courses at UCSD, Kobayashi emphasizes that research is not a haphazard process. And the diving
scientist must face more challenges than the land scientist in
performing his research.

"Underwater research is a disciplined process. It is unique in
that the scientist has to be a diver in order to perform his research
projects," says Kobayashi. "It's not like working in a lab. The
diving scientist must be willing to put up with getting in the water
when conditions aren't ideal, with making one small step forward
at the expense of many hours of hard work underwater.

"But I wouldn't trade it for anything in the world," he says. "I
get to do all the things I love best, without the regular stresses of
an office or strictly academic life. I know I am a happier person
for it."

That happier attitude is helped by the number of ways in which
diving can assist the scientist in studying the undersea world.
Although the research diver brings a vast array of knowledge
underwater with him, one cannot successfully study a reef or a
fish without meeting it on its own terms.

Perhaps it is discovered that fire worms are eating fire coral.
If the worms continue, the fire coral will die. This would have an
impact on a large shallow reef area that serves as home to millions of marine organisms. The marine biologist employs diving
as the tool for studying the problem and formulating the solution.

Diving is used in research observation. Firsthand observation
of the situation is the only way to begin. The marine biologist may
try to observe the fire worms in action or even tag them, though
it is pretty difficult to catch a worm. However, just as the land
scientist must record his observations, so a marine biologist must
do the same.

Secondly, diving is used in long-term monitoring. Since one
cannot bring the ocean into the laboratory, repeated visits are
necessary to check on equipment left in place for photographing.

When the research diver uses experimental manipulation, he
or she adds to or subtracts from the existing undersea environ-

ment in order to determine side effects. For example, what would happen if there was an oil spill in the shallow-water reef? How would the loss of life in the reef affect the fish and organisms in the surrounding area?

Marine biologists use diving as a tool in sample gathering, or gathering organisms they wish to study. Sometimes scuba tanks do double duty. Not only do they provide air for the research diver, but with a few manipulations, a tank can serve as a type of underwater vacuum. Vacuuming is particularly handy for dealing with the small, jellylike organisms that would be difficult to pick up with bare hands.

Underwater photography is essential to the marine biologist for two main reasons. Photos taken of a marine community can be enlarged and studied more effectively on land, with the aid of

A research diver, using a quadrapod camera system, surveys bottom-dwelling organisms. The quadrapod is an aluminum frame for holding a Nikonos camera and two strobe lights in place to photograph a small section of the ocean bottom.   JON D. WITMAN

good light and magnifying glasses. Time-lapse photography allows the marine biologist to study marine animals in their usual behavior patterns, without being affected by the presence of the diver.

Finally the advent of deep-sea submersibles has allowed marine biologists to study underwater communities never before accessible to scuba-diving scientists.

Dr. Jon Witman started as a sport diver when he was in high school. He knew from his summer and after-school work at the Sandy Hook Marine Laboratory near his home in New Jersey that marine biology was where he would devote his energies. Now a research associate at the Marine Science and Maritime Studies Center for Northeastern University, Dr. Witman has lived in the Hydrolab underwater habitat for two weeks and uses submersibles for deep-water observations.

"We know very little about what's offshore because it has always been hard to work in deep water," he says. But thanks to submersibles and underwater video cameras, marine researchers are beginning to study marine communities and problems that affect our everyday lives.

"Stocks of commercially exploited fish are rapidly diminishing. We are definitely overfishing our waters, but we don't understand the ecosystems well enough to construct a food web."

Understanding the environment and food chain of the cod and haddock—both fish used for human consumption—might prevent the two popular fish from becoming endangered species. This would benefit both the commercial fisherman and the fish lover.

Overfishing is just one of the problems marine biologists are studying. Dr. Lindberg's research on the ecology of coral reefs will provide oil companies with information about the effects of

◀ Using a suction device, marine scientists collect samples of tiny organisms from the coral reefs off the Florida coast. Underwater biologists must still take notes—on divers' slates. FLORIDA INSTITUTE OF TECHNOLOGY

oil spills on the marine population and whether their offshore equipment can serve as an artificial reef for millions of other marine animals.

"Different diving situations require different levels of technology. The scientist must determine what data he or she needs and what technology can best supply that data," Dr. Lindberg says. "Reefs are difficult to sample from the surface—you have large open spans and deep crevices and holes. You could try hook and line, but then your results are dependent on the skill of the fisherman. A net is impractical because you would miss so much. Sometimes being present as a diver with bubbles floating everywhere causes the fish to react to you, so we use a combination of techniques—saturation diving at around three hundred feet, underwater video cameras that can sweep an area and replay it for observation, and regular scuba diving at shallower depths."

Another kind of diving scientist is involved in the rescue of marine animals and maintaining the marine ecology of an area through support services.

Don Chittick is aquarium director for Sea World at its Marine Science and Conservation Center on Long Key, Florida. Part of the Marine Mammal Stranding Network, the center is called upon to rescue everything from beached whales to turtles or sharks in trouble. It is also responsible for the collection and breeding of animals for the Sea World parks in both Orlando and San Diego.

"One of our big functions is to provide support services for marine biologists working on projects," he says. "For example, Dr. Dan O'Dell from the University of Miami is studying the effects of oil spills on sea turtles. We set up the tanks for the hatchlings, monitor them for disease, and manipulate their environment to study the effects of the oil on the turtle population."

Yet another kind of diving scientist is the aquaculture specialist. Aquaculture, the art and science of raising plants and animals in a water environment, has been considered the means of combating fish overkill in our oceans. It is also being looked upon as a survival tool for Third World countries.

Both the University of Florida and Florida Institute of Technology, among others, have departments devoted totally to this emerging science. While underwater sea farms inspire the image of divers happily raking and harvesting the ocean floor, most aquaculture is accomplished in shallow water tanks or in ponds with floating platforms. The research diver may initially use diving as the tool for firsthand ecological observation and for continued maintenance of the underwater pens, but diving is less important in this discipline than in the mainstream marine biology / ecology.

Since marine biology / ecology is a research discipline, undergraduate academic training is available at various universities around the country. Institutions such as Woods Hole Oceanographic Institution in Massachusetts and Scripps Institute of Oceanography in California provide graduate and research forums for projects which are both privately and federally funded.

A few institutions provide specialized training that combines marine biology, marine ecology, and research diving techniques and methods in an unusual program for both undergraduates and graduate students as well as professionals from other fields.

Northeastern University and the University of Oregon, in a joint sponsorship, offer a year of study entitled the East / West Program. Qualified students go to three different locales during the year for classes and research diving. Fall is spent exploring the coastal and nearshore waters of the Pacific Northwest. Students are based at the Oregon Institute of Marine Biology, where they take courses in coastal biology, comparative physiology, marine botany, and several other facets of marine science.

Winter sends the students to Jamaica for a study of the diversity of coral reefs of the West Indies. Students travel to Discovery Bay Marine Laboratory, where they use diving techniques to study reef ecology, tropical terrestrial ecology, and the biology of fishes.

The final phase of the program brings the students to Northeastern University's Marine Laboratory in Nahant, a rocky peninsula north of Boston. Students take courses in benthic ecology (the ecology of ocean bottom–dwelling organisms) and animal behavior, among others. Current research techniques are taught and applied to independent research diving projects.

"While we don't require that the students be certified divers at the time of registration, we strongly suggest that they already be certified," says Morgan Hardwick-Witman, coordinator of the program.

In addition to the full-year program, Northeastern offers a summer marine biology / ecology program, available to everyone, with faculty members from Woods Hole and Harvard University also in attendance. This program teaches diving research methods in addition to biological oceanography and related courses.

The University of California at San Diego also offers a wide range of marine ecology / diving research courses. Students can learn to dive and receive their certifications at UCSD as well as prepare for work in the marine sciences.

There are four primary areas of employment for those interested in the marine biology / ecology field: education, research, the private sector, and industry.

The largest avenue of employment for the new marine biologist / ecologist is in the area of education. Teachers are needed for elementary and middle school, high school, and college. Who could sleep through a science class devoted to the colorful world under the sea, complete with slides, shells, coral, and stories garnered firsthand through diving?

While elementary and high school science teachers prepare themselves for a general curriculum, colleges and universities allow the marine biologist to deal only with his specialty. A growing number of universities enable coordination between the science department and diver-training programs so that serious students can get firsthand experience in underwater research and methods.

The second largest forum for marine biologists / ecologists is

research. There are a number of institutions around the world that sponsor research projects or provide the technology and personnel for government research projects.

The National Oceanic and Atmospheric Administration is part of the U.S. Department of Commerce. Based in Rockville, Maryland, its primary marine responsibilities are fisheries, ocean services, seafloor properties and processes, and combating pollution. NOAA recognized the need for an undersea research program in 1971, then reorganized to expand the program in 1980. Today, NOAA's research projects employ state-of-the-art technology to enable scientists to work more efficiently under the sea. One applies for employment with NOAA through government personnel systems.

NOAA's Office of Undersea Research supports NOAA's underwater mission by providing undersea equipment and facilities to extend the ability of marine researchers beyond the limits of traditional laboratory and ship-based research. Its specific objectives are to: acquire scientific information about the marine ecology and environments in U.S. coastal waters; broaden support of research efforts requiring advanced undersea facilities; provide training and facilities to develop a cadre of scientists proficient in advanced underwater techniques; and strengthen academic relations with NOAA in accomplishing marine research.

Projects and activities include the Caribbean Regional Hydrolab; deep-sea submersibles; extension programs at the Universities of Hawaii, North Carolina, and Southern California; diving research and development; and the encouragement of joint international and interagency research projects.

Scripps Institute of Oceanography; Woods Hole Institution; Harbor Branch Foundation in Ft. Pierce, Florida; and the Smithsonian Institution all have extensive research programs for the qualified scientist. Projects range from the study of deep-sea bacteria and the transformation of hydrocarbons to the energy transfer of wave motion and the location of the *Titanic*.

Another area of employment for the diving scientist is the private sector. Engineering consulting firms are increasingly called upon to look at water pollutants and both chemical and temperature changes in the water. Most of this information is needed for community studies and by companies wishing to build or develop waterfront land.

Industry can also provide employment for the marine biologist / ecologist as major oil companies make increasingly large expenditures to drill in the deep ocean. For example, if one of the oil-drilling platforms becomes fouled underwater, a marine biologist is called in to investigate. He might discover that marine creatures are using the underwater structure as a home.

The American Academy of Underwater Sciences was organized in 1977 to provide the scientific diving community with a means of exchanging information on scientific diving. It is concerned with diving safety, state-of-the-art scientific diving techniques, and research diving expeditions. It provides a link among scientific divers from fifty-nine countries and offers a forum for news on topics ranging from new techniques and safety to research projects and employment. As the scientific diving industry grows, so does the membership, which includes sixty-six scientific and undersea federations.

So as humans begin to discover that their lives and the life of their planet is dependent upon the ocean, the need and opportunity for undersea research will demand that more marine biologists and ecologists be trained. We hope they will learn—and teach us—how to maintain the ocean so it will continue to provide the things we take for granted.

12

DIVER MEDIC

The emergency call comes in to the dive center at 10:15 A.M. A fireman, who has been fighting a blaze at an industrial plant, has been found facedown and unconscious in the basement of the building. Smoke inhalation—carbon dioxide poisoning—is the culprit.

Medical authorities determine the most efficient treatment for the fireman is a hyperbaric chamber. And the dive center has the chamber. Can they bring him in?

Yes, hurry.

Divers and students appear in the vast room, dominated by the huge, cylindrical white chamber that simulates the pressure exerted on the body when diving. Gas levels are checked. Medical equipment is laid out. The diver medic, Bill Bensky, smoothly coordinates first-aid preparation, chamber readiness, and communications with physicians at the nearby hospital.

Within thirty minutes, a blue and white police helicopter lands on the center's pad. The fireman is carried in by fellow fire fighters.

And then the diver medic takes over.

Accompanying the unconscious fireman into the chamber, he performs a quick examination. The chamber's door slams shut with the finality of a submarine's escape hatch. The medic keeps up the communication through the chamber's audio system and clear portholes. The pressure is on . . . in more ways than one. They are "going down" to at least sixty-six feet of seawater pressure.

"He has 60 percent carbon dioxide in his blood level. . . . We can't clear his ears. . . . I'm going to try Valium. If that doesn't work, we'll have to puncture his eardrums surgically to relieve the pressure. . . . The Valium's working."

Firemen are milling around. The fire commissioner, remembering too many men lost to smoke inhalation, is somber. There are whispers. "Yes, his family's been told. . . . on their way . . . How are they going to get rid of that CO_2? That stuff kills. . . ."

Then comes the voice from within the chamber. "He's waking up!"

It is 12:15 P.M., only an hour and a half after the victim's arrival. If left to the natural order of things, the fireman's body would not have thrown off the amount of carbon dioxide he had inhaled for another two days, if ever.

In the hyperbaric chamber, under pressure, his body was flushed with oxygen, forcing the poisonous carbon dioxide out of his system. He was sitting up and talking when they carried him out two hours after his arrival, for transport to the hospital.

Diver medic Bill Bensky's day is not always as dramatic as this, but as hyperbaric chambers are becoming more widely used for everything from diving-related accidents to treatment of burn infections and multiple sclerosis, the medic's job becomes more diverse. In addition to coordinating emergency efforts involving hyperbaric chambers, the diver medic can be found handling crises on oil-rig platforms, teaching first aid in a dive shop, or being called upon at resort areas.

The diver medic is not a medical doctor. His training is usually obtained through commercial dive schools offering this specialty or through one of the sport-diving schools such as PADI, which offers a rescue-diver rating.

Why is there a need for the diver medic? Injuries from sport diving or commercial diving present a unique problem for the emergency medical system. While there are relatively few injuries in sport diving, considering the millions who now dive, the injuries that are incurred are frequently such that they require immediate attention. Also, offshore dive sites are usually so isolated that it becomes mandatory that competent medical care be available on the scene to handle any type of diving or industrial accident until direct communication with a physician can be established.

Though these are real areas of medical need, they do not present a sufficient health hazard to support a physician full-time. This situation has led to the advent of the diver medic.

Bensky, medical director for the Professional Diving School of New York, is also rated as a physician's assistant and holds an undersea technology degree. In addition to directing the use of the school's hyperbaric chamber (which includes the regular weekly treatments of patients referred by hospitals), he teaches others to be medics.

"There is a real need for medics because M.D.s can't afford to handle diving full-time," he says. "There is also a growing awareness of the benefits of the hyperbaric chamber in this country. Trauma centers are now using them. The chamber reduces swelling in the brain and helps with the healing of wounds and skin grafts."

Responsibilities of the diver medic vary with the job setting. Very basically, a medic would administer first aid and cardiopulmonary resuscitation.

"More specifically, the medic might also have to start intrave-

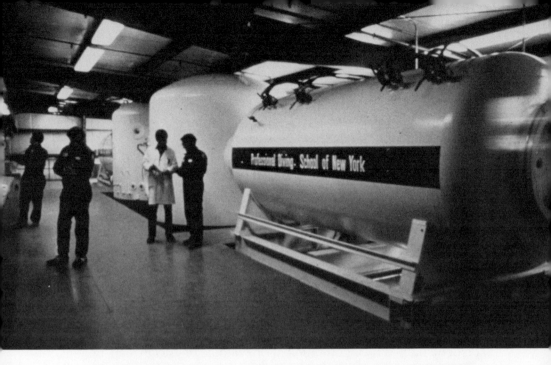

Hyperbaric chambers such as this one at the Professional Diving School of New York not only help divers recover from accidents but are being used to aid people suffering from smoke inhalation, burns, and multiple sclerosis. GARY PARSONS / PROFESSIONAL DIVING SCHOOL OF NEW YORK

nous lines, administer drugs, do neurological exams, and handle all phases of pre-emergency care," says Reed Bohn, Jr., diver medic for The Ocean Corporation. "Most diver-medic training courses include working for hospital emergency rooms as part of the preparation."

Diver medics depart from regular emergency medics in that they must also be able to recognize and handle those injuries specifically related to diving. This can include air embolisms—air bubbles in the blood—and the bends.

Then there are the more subtle problems of physiological stress and psychological stress. Physiological stress can take the form of fatigue, seasickness, cramps, and adverse reaction to cold. Psychological stress at a mild level can be as simple as nervousness before a dive. To some degree, stress is present in all dives. But a diver who is particularly stressed can panic underwater, endangering his life and the lives of others.

When employed on an offshore oil rig or power plant, the diver medic may be called upon to handle situations that are really construction-related rather than diver-related. Just as paramedical personnel on land construction sites can be called upon to handle cuts, burns, electric shocks, or crushed limbs caused by falling beams, so can the diver medic. However, the diver medic will often have to begin treatment in the water. He will have to know how to move an injured person from water to dry land (and communicate those directions underwater) and then take proper first-aid action.

Obviously, the advantage to having a trained diver medic on site is that not only does the injured diver receive immediate attention, but the medic can then communicate effectively with a physician located some distance from the site.

Because of the growth of both the sport- and commercial-

A diver medic records his patient's vital signs inside the hyperbaric chamber. Diver medics provide the treatment necessary in emergency situations when physicians are not available. THE OCEAN CORPORATION

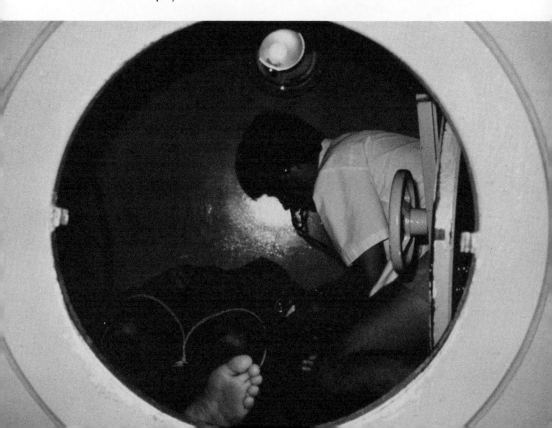

diving industries, and the limited number of hyperbaric chambers and trained personnel, the Divers Alert Network was formed in 1980. DAN operates a twenty-four-hour national hot line to provide advice on early treatment, evacuation, and hyperbaric treatment of diving-related injuries. In an emergency, a diver or medic can speak to a diving medicine–trained physician. Additionally, DAN provides diving safety information to help prevent accidents.

"DAN also collects data on diving injuries and the effectiveness of treatment," says Chris Wacholz, assistant director of DAN. "Without this kind of collective clinical information, we would never be able to identify good or bad methods of treatment, analyze the results of treatment for different kinds of injuries, or propose new and safer ways to dive and treat diving injuries."

Recommendations from DAN on the treatment of diving injuries are included in diver-medic training programs. Other preparatory courses would include anatomy, physiology, shock, intravenous procedures, diver-rescue systems, trauma management, emergency medicine, and critical-care medicine.

"Diver medic is a great career choice for the person who enjoys diving and is interested in medicine but doesn't have the inclination to go the whole medical route," says Reed Bohn.

Some say being a diver medic is the best of both worlds.

13

PHYSICIAN DIVER

Joe Diver has just returned from a fabulous dive vacation in the Florida Keys, but all is not well. While attempting to make a deep dive with a group, he experienced sharp pain in his left ear. The ocean was very choppy that day, and as the rest of the divers descended quickly to escape being tossed about on the surface, Joe spent his time changing his depth, pinching his nose, and blowing hard to try to clear his ears. He finally just plunged downward, hoping his ears would clear themselves. They did not.

Eventually he gave up and went back to the dive boat. He caught a plane home that afternoon and almost cried out in pain during the flight. His ear still hurt. Aspirin failed to calm the intensity of the pain. Unable to hear with his left ear and feeling dizzy, Joe visited his family physician the next day. Unfamiliar with diving physiology, the doctor examined Joe's ears, told him he probably had the beginnings of an ear infection caused by bacteria in the water, and sent him home with antibiotics.

Jennifer, too, is not feeling well after a dive vacation for which she spent the entire year saving. Wanting to see as much as possible as she vacationed in the glorious azure waters of the Hawaiian islands, she signed up for two dives a day with various dive shops on three different islands. Having been a certified diver for five years, she confidently told all the dive masters that she knew her decompression tables and was looking forward to making some deep dives.

Unfortunately, after the first couple of days, she began to experience fatigue and a slight aching in her joints. But that didn't stop Jennifer. After all, arthritis ran in her family, and she didn't want to waste a minute of dive time. So she made another dive —a deep one. As the dive drew to a close, her attention was caught by a large colorful fish heading for the surface. Trying to get one last picture, Jennifer darted after it. As she broke the surface, she passed out. Fortunately, she was rescued before she could drown.

Sam Diver also brought a souvenir of his dive trip home to Denver with him—in his hand. Sam made a night dive for the first time, marveling at the incredible marine life that came out of the corals to socialize after the sun went down. Forgetting his gloves, he winced slightly as his hands brushed against the sharp coral crevices and sea creatures that loomed out of the dark at him.

By the time he made it home, Sam was running a slight temperature and infection had set in. His family physician gave him a broad-spectrum antibiotic but, unfamiliar with diving and marine life, didn't probe deep enough to find a toxic sliver of a sea urchin's spine still embedded in Sam's hand.

When one thinks of diving accidents or problems, one tends to envision the worst possible scenario—the shark attack, a diver coughing up blood or drowning, or the diver with the air embolism which explodes in the brain shortly after the diver surfaces. These are the exceptions rather than the rule. Most medical dive problems are difficult to detect because the divers are walking around and functioning but feeling ill or experiencing increasing pain.

For this reason, there is a growing need for physicians trained in diving medicine who can correctly diagnose a diving-related medical problem and prescribe the proper course of action.

Although there has been tremendous growth in sport diving, that growth has not been reflected in the number of physicians trained to handle injuries related to diving.

The reasons for this are twofold. First, unlike tennis, jogging, or even football, which are spectator sports easily viewed, understood, and participated in, diving still carries an aura of mystery. Special instruction and equipment are needed. The diver goes into a foreign environment. And there are no crowds cheering the diver on to victory. It is easy to diagnose stress to the knees or ankles of a runner, fractured ribs in the body of a football player, or strained muscles in the back or arm of a tennis player. You can usually see the injuries occur—and where and why they occur.

Not so in diving.

Secondly, the physician himself has probably played tennis or football, or jogged, so he can identify with the patient. He understands the environment and stresses the patient has faced and, with that extra edge, can accurately make a diagnosis and prescribe a successful course of treatment.

Not so with diving.

According to the Divers Alert Network and the Undersea Medical Society (UMS), there are only approximately two thousand physicians trained in diving medicine. Since the numbers involved in the sport are relatively low, it is not yet recognized as a complete medical specialty such as orthopedics or even sports medicine. But the diving patient needs the physician diver.

In the case of Joe Diver, he was not suffering from an ear infection. He was suffering from middle-ear barotrauma caused by inadequate pressure equalization between the middle ear and the surrounding environment. Part of what contributed to Joe's problem with clearing his ears is that he has a constant sinus problem, which assisted in trapping air in the middle ear. Flying home in an airplane pressurized at approximately eight thousand feet only added to his problems. If left uncorrectly diagnosed and treated, Joe could have experienced permanent hearing loss.

Jennifer Diver did not have arthritis but a mild case of decompression sickness, which was aggravated by her continuing to dive. While the symptoms can sometimes imitate those of the common flu or a mild form of arthritis, the physician trained in diving medicine would be able to quickly zero in on the actual problem.

And finally, most lacerations received while diving are minor, but Sam's needed some special attention. Sea urchins cause many infections each year as divers make contact with them

Diving accidents can present unique physiological problems that can be most easily diagnosed and treated by diving physicians. PROFESSIONAL ASSOCIATION OF DIVING INSTRUCTORS

intentionally for photographs, or lean or step on them unintentionally. Although most pieces of the spine will disintegrate, a few of the more virulent ones will not and are a continuing source of infection if not removed.

Where can physicians get the specialized training needed? From four primary sources: The military holds training sessions for their personnel; the National Oceanic and Atmospheric Administration holds a three-week session each year; and both the Undersea Medical Society and Human Underwater Biology (HUB) sponsor continuous workshops and training sessions for American Medical Association credit.

Dedicated to recognizing diving medicine as a definitive specialty, presenting training seminars for physicians, and promoting professional and scientific communication, the Undersea Medical Society offers six levels of membership. They range from

Several courses are held throughout the country each year to train physicians in the particulars of diving medicine. PROFESSIONAL ASSOCIATION OF DIVING INSTRUCTORS

college student to physician to corporate members in forty-seven countries. Based in Bethesda, Maryland, UMS has a major interest in two closely related areas—one being the biomedical and physiological aspects of deep-sea diving, and the other, hyperbaric therapy of various diseases and conditions.

In addition to publishing journals and newsletters, UMS holds workshops for physicians who are expert in various specialties to discuss the diverse aspects of diving medicine. Examples of recent topics include: thermal problems in diving, early diagnosis of decompression sickness, interaction of drugs with the hyperbaric environment, and effects of diving during pregnancy.

Also presenting workshops throughout the year, but with the enticing twist of exotic locales all over the world, is HUB, based in San Antonio, Texas. Headed by Dr. Bruce Bassett, HUB provides a package of exciting dive trips for the physician and his family, combined with classroom seminar work and on-site demonstrations by noted medical authorities.

Bassett, a twenty-three-year veteran of the air force, trained in aerospace medicine and the author of the diving-curriculum manual for the air force, began HUB in 1977 when he saw that the growth of sport diving was not matched by a growth in the medical community's knowledge of the sport's potential health hazards.

Among those enrolling in HUB's Doctorfish program are family physicians, cardiologists, emergency-room physicians, and dentists. If a physician does not know how to dive prior to the workshop, a certification course is arranged on site.

"I firmly believe that we are contributing to the safety of the sport-diving community—that's the missionary aspect of this kind of program," says Bassett. "The only way we can keep the sport self-regulated is through diver education . . . and physician education."

14

UNDERWATER ARCHAEOLOGIST

The Civil War had broken out. The Union wanted a ship that would control the waters and put the Confederacy in its place. So the navy accepted the design of Swedish engineer-inventor John Ericsson. He gave them the *Monitor.*

The *Monitor* was a radical departure from conventional warships, made of iron rather than wood. She was powered by a steam engine, used a screw propeller rather than a paddle wheel, and sported a revolving gun turret—the first of its kind.

She went head-to-head with the Confederacy's pride, the steamship *Merrimac,* at Hampton Roads, Virginia, on March 9, 1862, but the battle was little contest for the armored vessel. No one stood in her way. She did indeed rule the northern waters for the Union government.

But she couldn't battle Mother Nature. By late 1862, she was resting upside down on that famous gun turret, in 270 feet of water. She was put there by a storm, sixteen miles off Cape Hatteras, North Carolina.

Like the *Monitor*'s, their names reach out from their watery graves like tombstones drawing us back to those storm-battered shores: the *Emperor,* a regal freighter which broke up on a reef in Lake Superior, Michigan; the *America,* wrecked in a snowstorm off Isle Royale, Michigan, December 1906; and even the nameless ship which sailed from Syria in 1400 B.C. and crashed into a reef of jagged rocks before it could reach its destination. Scattered between 140 and 170 feet of water off Kas, Turkey, it is thought to be the oldest Bronze Age underwater excavation to date.

As important as the unveiling of the Egyptian pharaohs' tombs, the discovery, mapping, cataloging, and preservation of the thousands of shipwrecks, which give us keys to human history, is the forte of the underwater archaeologist.

The field of underwater archaeology owes its birth to the development of scuba gear that enables divers to stay down long enough to investigate the wrecks of mighty ships. The underwater archaeologist is something of a detective who searches the remains of a ship for clues to peoples, cultures, or even the cause of the wreck.

While many might confuse the underwater archaeologist with the treasure hunter or salvor, the profession is characterized by scientific study and procedure. Where other subcategories of archaeology are distinguished by geographical descriptions, such as Egyptian archaeology, or southwestern archaeology, the only description which sets this field apart is its environment—the water.

Combining skills in classical archaeology, maritime history, marine salvage, and anthropology, the underwater archaeologist has as his playground the underwater world, which covers three-fourths of our globe. In addition to inner and outer continental shelves under the seas, archaeological sites exist in inland waterways, lakes, and submerged caves. Shipwrecks, subject to strong currents, are often broken up, and debris is carried by wave action to channels or riverbeds.

It is becoming apparent to scientists that a number of pieces to the puzzle of man in the New World are to be found underwater. In Florida, for example, a concentrated underwater archaeological effort has been directed toward the karst—or limestone bedrock—areas.

Try to imagine what it would be like if the ocean's water level were to be raised thirty feet. Much of what is now populated land would be underwater in most of our coastal cities. This appears to be what happened between what we consider prehistoric times and now. And underwater archaeologists are making many startling discoveries as they investigate the karst. From underwater caves, which revealed ceremonial statues, to Wakulla Springs, Florida, where an entire mastodon skeleton was removed, to another karst where scientists found human brain material in a cranium believed to be several thousand years old, exciting things are happening in this growing field of underwater science.

Richard Brantley, an underwater archaeologist at Florida Institute of Technology, credits the real definition of the underwater archaeological field to Dr. George Bass, of Texas A & M University and director of the Institute of Nautical Archaeology (INA). It was Bass's struggles in the late 1960s to get nautical archaeology recognized as a legitimate discipline and his discovery of the startling Kas shipwreck that is bringing this area of scientific endeavor into the public and government eye.

Piecing together history—making people come alive at the bottom of the sea—is accomplished with painstaking effort and a variety of tools. Sonar, underwater metal detectors, air bags, flotation devices, and aluminum culverts to isolate one area under study without disturbing the surrounding sand are all utilized. Print cameras, remote sensing devices, and underwater video cameras allow the archaeologist to study the wreck site in great detail later.

But, like the land archaeologist, the most important tools for the underwater archaeologist are his brain and his hands, called into play in the "mudding" technique. With one hand firmly planting his body so he doesn't float away, the scientist uses the other to fan the water back and forth until a small hole in the sand or silt forms. Just as the gold prospector shifted sand until the heavier objects (gold) remained on the bottom, so too the underwater archaeologist shifts the sand to uncover what may lay beneath.

Working through the body of a wreck, the archaeologist is able to reconstruct an era. Playing the maritime historian, he or she might ask, "What is the significance of this wreck in history, and how does it relate to what is already known?" Studies of both literature and historical data reveal areas of wreck clustering due to recurrent storms or hostile rocks. Other reasons for wrecks include battles or simple failure of ship design.

From an anthropological perspective, the archaeologist might ask, "What do the artifacts at the site tell us about the human beings—their stresses, interactions, pastimes, food preferences, manner of dress, armaments, and health?" Often described as an underwater time capsule, a shipwreck can reveal the social strata of an age through the placement of the crew's quarters in relation to the officers'. Discovery of the ship's store allows a peek into diet, dress, and recreational pursuits of the era, while the surgery area offers a look at medical tools and needs.

The "architect" side of the underwater archaeologist's personality would investigate the ship's construction, use of shipbuilding materials, and propulsion characteristics; the "detective" tries to piece together the answers to all the questions while preserving what artifacts exist.

Problems faced by the underwater archaeologist in trying to reconstruct history come in two categories: nature and man.

The most obvious challenge comes from the sea itself. Time and wave action often fragment the ships, strewing them and their contents over miles of sand. What may be visible one day could be entirely encased in silt the next, and vice versa. Once a wreck, or the remains of a culture in an underwater cave, is discovered, the investigator faces the challenges of cold water, poor visibility, disintegrating wood, and of course the very fact that he or she is working underwater. Preservation techniques are still developing. Artifacts that may have sat underwater undisturbed for decades face oxidation and decay the moment they are brought to the surface.

But the biggest challenge to the underwater archaeologist comes from man—the treasure hunter, the salvage diver, the wreck diver who is more interested in a ship's lantern sitting on his mantel than in worrying about its historical significance.

Charged with the protection and management of our country's underwater resources is the National Park Service's Submerged Cultural Resources Unit (SCRU), headed by underwater archaeologist Dan Lenihan. Based in Santa Fe, New Mexico, the mobile diving unit is responsible for the archaeological investigation and cataloging of several hundred thousand acres of underwater property designated as the park service's historical shipwreck

A section of *Cumberland*'s paddle wheel is examined by a National Park Service ranger. *Cumberland* was lost off Isle Royale National Park in Lake Superior in 1877.   DAN LENIHAN / NATIONAL PARK SERVICE

areas. In some cases, they are dealing with wreck populations in the hundreds.

"A lot of park managers know they have shipwrecks, but they're often not priorities," says Lenihan, "because they have a whole range of other problems they're held accountable for by the park service."

But federal funds and public attention are converging on the nation's submerged wrecks as the realization dawns that preservation of a historical wreck is just as important as preservation of a significant building. While it would be unthinkable to allow treasure seekers to pull bricks off Independence Hall, legislation protecting underwater sites remains a controversy.

"Historic sites are potential sources of interest and enjoyment for the diving and nondiving public," says Lenihan. "A shipwreck

National Park Service archaeologist Dan Lenihan examines steam pump found in the wreckage of the *Henry Chisholm* (built in 1870, sunk 1898) off Isle Royale in Lake Superior.   LARRY MURPHY / NATIONAL PARK SERVICE

National Park Service divers map the remains of the *Monarch,* a wooden passenger / package vessel lost in a snowstorm off Isle Royale in 1906.   LARRY MURPHY / NATIONAL PARK SERVICE

is a magnificent thing to see, but there's nothing uglier than a wreck that has had everything that shines pulled off it to go on someone's mantelpiece.

"It's a change in ethic. Just as divers have learned to respect the natural environment—not to pull off sections of coral reef, for instance—there's no reason that the same ethic shouldn't be applied to shipwrecks."

Training in underwater archaeology can be accomplished at a number of universities. Texas A & M and East Carolina University are among the frontrunners in the development of underwater archaeological programs. Also dedicated to education, communication, and underwater archaeological projects worldwide—offering summer opportunities in fieldwork for students as well as for professionals—is the Institute of Nautical Archaeology (INA). Based at Texas A & M University, this nonprofit organization fosters the study of the history of seafaring. Projects have been sponsored in such diverse locations as the Mediterranean, Africa, the Far East, and the Caribbean as well as in the United States. Research projects require fieldwork and classroom, lab, and museum work, but membership in INA is open to the general public.

While past shipwreck finds have been the products of adventurers, the future holds a different kind of promise.

"We hope that an archaeologist fifty years from now will be able to reflect on a development that took place in the latter part of the twentieth century," says Lenihan, "wherein shipwreck studies were characterized by rich, interdisciplinary efforts conducted with the benefit of explicit research designs and a strong sensitivity for the fragile, nonrenewable nature of the resource."

15

POLICE SEARCH & RECOVERY

The murderer thinks he's going to get away with it. Blinding rage . . . loss of control . . . he's committed a crime. How to get rid of the gun? Running from the scene of blood and life ebbing from the body, he spies the river. Aha! The perfect place to toss the gun. Nobody will ever find one small gun in such a large, cold, dirty river. Snickering to himself, he throws as hard as he can and then hurries home to establish an alibi.

Two weeks later, he is in custody, charged with murder. And the weapon, with his fingerprints visible, is placed on the table before him. Recovered intact from that large, cold, dirty river.

The police unit responsible for the recovery is known by different names across the country, but it is essentially a search and recovery team. Using scuba gear and techniques in addition to very specialized training, these teams are increasingly called upon to recover everything from weapons or other items used to commit crimes, to automobiles and bodies.

As the scuba industry has grown and developed to the point where other disciplines and businesses have been able to utilize some aspect of underwater technology, so too have techniques been tailored to individual, specialized needs.

While the primary career of a member of a search and recovery team is with the police force, the diving team is being recognized and employed more as a specialty, just as the narcotics squad, vice squad, and juvenile units have their own identities. Because of police scuba teams, evidence that was once considered lost is now recovered a good percentage of the time, thereby increasing the successful prosecution of criminals.

In addition, the recovery of both lost items and bodies is also more and more successful as law-enforcement units upgrade their own training with skills modified to their own geographical locations. The recovery of a gun, for example, will involve a slightly different set of circumstances if a unit has to search the Hudson River as opposed to an inland waterway or lake.

At the time of this writing, there are only two full-time police search and recovery teams in the country, while most other police and sheriff's departments have a number of trained divers that they can mobilize when the need arises.

Lieutenant Robert Hayes, who heads Manhattan's Harbor Unit Underwater Recovery Team, has twenty diving officers on shift rotation twenty-four hours a day. Each officer is called upon to dive at least once a day, and the reasons are as diverse as the city of New York itself.

"People always ask me what is the most unusual recovery or situation we've been involved with," says Hayes, whose search responsibility includes some 576 square miles of water, "but what some people consider unusual is a regular day around here. For example, although there was a big shark scare a little while back, a plane crashed in the area and some of our divers got on a helicopter, jumped into the water, and recovered the airplane." A regular day.

Another time, a murder had occurred, and police units in six different areas had discovered pieces of the body. The harbor unit's task was to search underwater for the head. A normal day.

And when the president comes to town, it is the underwater recovery team that is charged with the responsiblity for surveying the piers and surrounding areas for bombs or other security problems prior to his arrival. The team has been trained on the presidential helicopter. All in a day's work.

Even seasoned pros shudder at one aspect of recovery work.

"Recovering bodies is the toughest thing," says Hayes soberly. "And recovering the body of a small child is the worst."

Whether in the big city or in suburban or rural areas, search

Officers on New York City's police search and recovery team work in shifts, round the clock, to uncover weapons used in crimes, provide security to visiting dignitaries, and recover bodies. HARBOR UNIT UNDERWATER RECOVERY TEAM

and recovery techniques involve a definite search pattern, with divers working in pairs or sometimes in groups of five.

Lieutenant Arthur O'Brien helped organize the Morris County, New Jersey, sheriff's department's Search and Recovery Unit. A cooperative effort among the county's law-enforcement officials, divers are pulled from many units when the need arises.

"The search patterns we use vary with the situation," says O'Brien, "but the most common one involves placing a five-foot grid on the bottom and methodically searching that one area. Then we flip the grid over and search the next five-foot area."

Other methods include a circle pattern, where an officer holds one end of a rope and another takes the opposite end, gradually swimming in a circle around him (most commonly used in searching for bodies), or the running jack, which involves ropes and five-man teams.

As if police work and crime solving weren't difficult enough on dry land, underwater police units have the additional challenges that only a foreign environment like water can present.

"Our number-one problem is pollution," says Hayes. "The city of New York dumps millions of gallons of raw sewage into the water every day. Because we have to dive in that, we have to take extraspecial precautions, like full-face masks which are pressurized, and allow underwater communication." The Harbor Unit also wears full dry suits to combat frigid temperatures. They must undergo thorough physical examinations at least twice a year to check for parasites and hepatitis.

Black-water diving, as O'Brien refers to it—that is, diving with little or no visibility—demands extra equipment in the form of high-intensity underwater lights.

"Sometimes we go down there and can't see past our out-stretched hands," says Hayes. Sometimes even the lights, boasting 100,000 candlepower, don't help.

The disintegration of evidence is a problem to be faced because of the corrosive powers of salt water and wave action. Depending upon what the object to be recovered is, fresh water can be just as detrimental. And then there are the currents, faced

Due to heavy pollution, police recovery-team divers who dive in New York's Hudson River must be completely covered and insulated by their suits. HARBOR UNIT UNDERWATER RECOVERY TEAM

more by teams working rivers and coastal areas than those working inland.

While O'Brien's suburban team is often called upon to recover stolen vehicles, Hayes sees underwater vehicles as an obstacle to be overcome while searching for other things.

"Anywhere in the city of New York where a person can drive a car up to the water's edge, there are cars in the water," he says. "Sometimes it really looks like a junkyard down there! Cars, concrete, cables, cans . . . you name it, we have to go around it."

Those interested in police work who would like to use their scuba skills in a professional capacity would do best to apply to the law-enforcement agency of their choice and then inquire about a search and recovery team. But the training, usually accomplished in-house, is stringent and thorough.

Personal interviews, medical examinations, and written tests are just a beginning. The applicant must already hold a national scuba certification and have some experience under his or her belt. Because of the adverse diving conditions under which these units work, the applicant must be sure that he can handle the water temperatures and the claustrophobic effect caused by diving in black water or being completely encased in a protective scuba suit.

An aptitude for mechanics is also helpful, as most units are called upon to maintain the boats used as well as to assist other government agencies in underwater repairs.

The ability to get along with others is important. Not only is the search and recovery specialist performing under the stress usually encountered by police officers, but he is also stressed by performing those duties underwater and sometimes in close quarters with other diving officers for hours at a time.

"I also look for someone who has guts," says Hayes. "The diver has to have the guts to jump out of a helicopter into the water, for example, or dive in the feel-it-before-you-see-it type of dirty water."

Continually developing training in the search and recovery units, coupled with the officers' training involving the handling of evidence and testifying in court, is making a dent in law enforcement's effectiveness.

"A lot of people who commit crimes think if they tossed the weapon in the water, they're off the hook," says Hayes.

Police search and recovery units are proving daily that it isn't so any longer.

16

THE MILITARY

When Xerxes, king of Persia from 486 to 465 B.C., developed his grand plan to conquer Greece, he pulled out all the stops. Not only did he amass an army from all corners of his kingdom, but he turned his sights to the sea. Ordering his strongest swimmers into the water, equipped with hollow reeds for breathing, he staged an attack on the Greeks on land and on the sea and under it. Xerxes lost the war—but he is credited with using the first combat divers in naval warfare.

Just as land-combat techniques have become more sophisticated since the time of sword and shield, so underwater combat has also grown because of the technological advancements in underwater equipment. In fact, the military—and the navy in particular—is given credit for much of the development and attention given to the diving industry today.

As with police search and recovery, the career here is the

navy, but within the navy are opportunities for those interested in diving. From the navy fleet diver, to the Explosive Ordnance Disposal (EOD) teams, to the very elite navy Seals, diving is used both in peace and in warfare in today's military.

Although training programs vary, health requirements are the same for all three categories of navy diver—one must be thirty years of age or younger at the time of enrollment in a dive training program and in top physical condition. In addition, the *Manual of Medicine and Surgery* from the Naval Special Warfare Training Department suggests that those aspiring to the Seals or underwater demolition teams prepare themselves well in advance for the rigorous training and testing. Preparation should include swimming regularly (concentrating on the breaststroke and sidestroke), running a mile in less than seven and a half minutes, and the following calisthenics, to be performed within two minutes each: thirty sit-ups, thirty push-ups, and six pull-ups.

Did your heart ever swell with pride as you watched our nation's fleet of ships and submarines cruising through the water? Anchors aweigh as the tall, sleek ships loaded with the latest in electronics and combat equipment take to the sea.

A navy fleet diver might see something else when watching the ships move out, however. Within his frame of reference are barnacles clogging up the machinery under the waterline, or the naval installations that must be constructed on the shore. He is the traditional hard-hat or deep-sea diver. The navy fleet diver, backbone of the navy's diving contingent, is responsible for underwater ship repair and maintenance, rescue and salvage operations, underwater construction, and experimental diving tasks. In short, he is the navy's equivalent of the commercial diver.

Currently, more than twelve hundred divers, classified according to five skill levels, serve on ships and at shore facilities throughout the world. The five skill levels that fall under the fleet diver umbrella are diver second-class, diver first-class, saturation diver, master diver, and medical deep-sea diving technician.

Diver second-class is the entry skill level in the program. A

A navy fleet diver, wearing an MK XII helium and oxygen rig, works with a hydraulic grinder in Hawaiian waters.   UNITED STATES NAVY

twelve-week course teaches basic diving skills including scuba, MK I Band Mask (a lightweight, surface-supplied air mask), and MK XII Diving System (surface-supplied hard-hat equipment). The course also covers physical fitness, diving physiology, and introduction to ship salvage and underwater cutting and welding.

Upon completion of training, graduates are normally assigned either to a rescue and salvage ship or to a submarine rescue ship for a two-year tour to develop rating skills and gain diving experience. The remainder of each diver's four-year sea tour of duty is usually spent aboard a tender, or repair ship. During this time, the second-class diver learns underwater hull repair and maintenance skills.

Diver first-class is the first level of advanced training in the diver program. After one year's experience as a second-class diver, those qualifying may apply for this additional training. The seventeen-week course, conducted at the navy's Diving and Salvage Training Center in Panama City, Florida, emphasizes supervisory skills used in diving operations. It teaches advanced ship-salvage techniques, submarine rescue, advanced underwater welding, demolitions, and ship husbandry skills (such as hull cleaning, propeller changes, and valve removals).

First-class divers continue the sea / shore rotations they started as second-class divers, and they are assigned to diving-capable ships, mobile diving and salvage units, ship repair activities, and instructor positions requiring advanced diver skills.

Saturation diver is the most advanced diver skill level. After a minimum of one year's experience as a first-class diver or diving medical technician, those qualifying may apply for saturation-diver training. The seventeen-week course increases the diver's knowledge of deep-diving systems, including the pressurized diving habitat. This system can support open-ocean diving to 850 feet. Upon completion of training, saturation divers are assigned to the Navy Experimental Diving Unit, diving research activities, or saturation-diving ships.

Master diver is the top of the fleet-diver line. The master diver supervises various, often complex, diving operations. Those with a minimum of two years' first-class or saturation-diver experience may apply for the five-week master diver evaluation. Those who are selected may be assigned to a variety of diving-capable ships or shore activities.

Finally, the medical deep-sea diving technician is a classification for navy corpsmen. Similar to the diver first-class training, training for this skill level prepares corpsmen to medically support diving operations.

Navy fleet divers receive additional diving pay ranging from

$100 per month for second-class divers to $300 per month for master divers.

The Explosive Ordnance Disposal consists of a small group of highly skilled volunteers, officers, and enlisted men. They are trained to detect, identify, render safe, and dispose of all types of U.S. and foreign explosive ordnance (military materials or equipment, including weapons). These may range from the simplest to the most complex missiles and bombs, wherever they may be causing a hazard on land or sea.

The full training course for Explosive Ordnance Disposal is forty-nine weeks long, with advanced training offered to those who qualify. Before entering the EOD, navy students must successfully complete the school's surface curriculum, which is given at the Redstone Arsenal in Alabama. There they learn about chemical and biological weapons. Then comes training in the basics of explosives and their effects, applied physical principles, electricity, batteries, and mechanical tools. They study manuals on the design, function, and hazardous components of explosive ordnances.

Navy students go through diver training at the Panama City facility and then receive eleven weeks of underwater ordnance instruction at Indian Head, Maryland. Since careless or inaccurate work could cost lives, precision and safety are emphasized in this technical area.

Instruction comes in the form of hands-on problems in which the students are given scenarios requiring them to identify and render safe an explosive device. These exercises are the core of EOD training. They take the student out of the classroom and put him under the pressure of a life-threatening situation where speed and accuracy are needed. On land, the students work on "dead," or inert, training devices. Underwater, however, each device is rigged with a half-pound block of TNT that explodes about twenty-five feet away if the student makes a mistake that would have caused a live explosive to detonate. It is a technique designed to keep students on their toes—or fins.

When trying to locate an underwater explosive, the diver's movements must be slow and deliberate rather than quick and jerky, so he does not bump into the explosive by accident. This can be particularly difficult in water with low visibility.

Once the basic training is completed, students are moved to the Patuxent River, where instructors have planted explosive devices. Working in teams, the students must locate the devices. Then they return to the surface, identify the devices in their manuals, and establish the proper "render safe" procedures. They must then return to the devices and successfully perform the techniques described.

Those graduating from the rigorous EOD program can be assigned to one of the more than sixty duty stations available around the world. Extra diving pay for EOD technicians ranges from $100 to $175 per month, plus additional incentives for demolition skills.

The Seals is the name of the navy's combat team that is cloaked in secrecy. They are called in to do the missions that others cannot—quietly, professionally, quickly—often under cover of night.

Their birth arose from tragedy: The date was November 20, 1942. The place, the Japanese-held island of Tarawa. Landing craft carrying troops from the Second Marine Battalion went aground on a submerged coral reef about 1,500 yards from the beach. The heavily laden marines began to wade to shore, but the holes in the ocean floor proved to be as lethal as enemy gunfire. Hundreds drowned and hundreds went down under enemy fire—easily picked off as they struggled toward land.

To provide more efficient water assaults and to eliminate the hazards to those attacking from the water, the navy Combat Demolition Teams were formed. Today, the Basic Underwater Demolition / Seal Teams are the elite naval combat units. They deploy small units of highly trained frogmen worldwide to support conventional operations by carrying out clandestine missions in enemy-held areas.

Taking their name from the elements—*sea, air, land*—the Seals are capable of swimming submerged for hours and can parachute at night to approach a target. They are trained to conduct small-unit reconnaissance patrols, intelligence-gathering missions, demolition raids, and many other combat-related tasks with little support. Not surprisingly, Seal training is the most rigorous the navy has to offer, and 50 percent of those who begin training never make it to graduation.

Seal training begins at the Naval Amphibious Base, Coronado, San Diego. It is tough on the body and the mind. The aspiring Seal must be able to endure twenty-three weeks of being wet, cold, tired, and hungry, including little or no sleep or rest during "Hell Week." The trainee's future in special warfare begins with a physical fitness screening. The test starts with a 300-yard, 7.5-minute swim. One of the basic underwater recovery strokes—the breaststroke or sidestroke—must be used.

During a ten-minute break, applicants change into shirts, long trousers, and high-top boots. They then must complete thirty sit-ups, thirty push-ups, and six pull-ups with palms facing out-ward, in two-minute time periods. A two-minute break is allowed between each exercise.

The final test is a 1-mile, 7.5-minute run in long trousers and high boots. Soldiers are dressed for combat and must be able to perform under those conditions.

Master Chief Storekeeper Dennis Drady is the East Coast in-service recruiter for special warfare. Despite the popular notion that Seals must be Charles Atlas types, he says that a man's size is not important. Only five feet three inches tall, Drady says that Seal training can produce a warrior capable of ten times the physical output ordinarily believed possible.

"We're looking for the best—that means academically, physically, mentally. We're not looking for the superjock. We're looking for the guy we can count on when the countin' counts."

During the second phase of Seal training, students are taught combat swimming techniques. They become expert in using scuba gear and specialized diving gear that generates few exhaust bubbles so they can't be detected. Students also learn how to treat diving-related disorders.

Finally, phase three consists of eight weeks of training in land warfare operations, patrolling, ambush techniques, weapons, explosives, and other tactics. As with the other two categories of navy diver, the Seals also receive extra diving pay of approximately $175 per month and special duty and hazard pay when called upon.

Basic Underwater Demolition / Seal Teams are to be found around the world, from Arctic demolition sites to space-shot recoveries in the Pacific. "For the individual who really wants something that's challenging, different, and rewarding," says Drady, "this is the only place to be."

SCHOOLS FOR TRAINING

SPORT DIVING

The following is a list of national certification and trade organizations offering training in the area of sport diving. Organizations must be consulted for individual program requirements and specialties. Or visit your local dive shop or YMCA for further information.

National Association of Scuba
  Diving Schools (NASDS)
Instructors College
4004 Sports Arena Boulevard
San Diego, CA 92110
(619) 224-3228
Executive Director: John
  Gaffney

National Association of
  Underwater Instructors
  (NAUI)
P.O. Box 14650
Montclair, CA 91763
(714) 621-5801
Executive Director: Marshall
  McNott

Professional Association of
  Diving Instructors (PADI)
International College
1243 East Warner Avenue
Santa Ana, CA 92705
(800) 235-3434
Dean / Executive Director:
  Commander James Williams

Progressive Sales Seminars
2215 East Colonial Drive
Orlando, FL 32803
(305) 896-4541
President: Hal Watts

Scuba Schools International (SSI)
2619 Canton Court
Ft. Collins, CO 80525
(303) 482-0883
Executive Director: Ed Christini

YMCA Scuba Program
Oakbrook Square
6083-A Oakbrook Parkway
Norcross, GA 30093
(404) 662-5172
Director: Millard Freeman

*Offering an academic program
  in addition to sport-diving
  specialty ratings:*

Florida Institute of Technology
  (FIT)
Sport Diving Operations
1707 Northeast Indian River
  Drive
Jensen Beach, FL 33457
(305) 334-4200

University of California, San
  Diego
Department of Physical
  Education, C–017
La Jolla, CA 92093
(619) 452-4037

COMMERCIAL DIVING

Coastal School of Deep Sea
  Diving
320 29th Avenue
Oakland, CA 94601
(415) 532-4211

College of Oceaneering
(Offers Associate in Applied
  Science degree)
(A division of Oceaneering
  International, Inc.)
Los Angeles Harbor
272 South Fires Avenue
Wilmington, CA 90744-6399
(213) 834-2501

Commercial Diving Institute
151–19 Powells Cove
  Boulevard
Whitestone, NY 11357
(718) 767-7800

Divers Academy
2500 Broadway
Camden, NJ 08104
(609) 966-1871

Divers Institute of Technology
(DIT)
4601 Shilshole Avenue
Northwest
P.O. Box 70312
Seattle, WA 98107
(206) 783–5542

The Ocean Corporation (TOC)
5709 Glenmont
Houston, TX 77081
(713) 661–0033

Professional Diving School of
New York (PDSNY)
(A division of International
Underwater Contractors)
222 Fordham Street
City Island, NY 10464
(212) 885–0600

Underwater Vehicle Training
Center (UVTC)
(A division of International
Underwater Contractors)
10046 Chickasaw Lane
Houston, TX 77041
(713) 690–0405 or (800)
IUC–ROVS

PROFESSIONAL INSTITUTES

Human Underwater Biology
(HUB)
Medical Seminars Inc.
8600 Wurzbach
Suite 1201
San Antonio, TX 78240
(512) 692–3535 or (800)
547–3747
President: Dr. Bruce Bassett

Institute of Nautical
Archaeology (INA)
P.O. Drawer AU
College Station, TX 77840
(409) 845–6694

Scripps Institute of
Oceanography
La Jolla, CA 92093
(619) 452–4445

Woods Hole Oceanographic
Institution
Woods Hole, MA 02543
(617) 548–1400

Universities offering a marine science curriculum (current lists can be obtained from school guidance counselors): University of Alaska; University of California, San Diego; Florida State University; University of Hawaii; Johns Hopkins University; Louisiana State University; University of Maine; Massachusetts Institute of Technology; University of Miami; University of Michigan; University of North Carolina; Northeastern University; Oregon State

University; University of Rhode Island; Scripps Institute; University of Southern California; Texas A & M; Virginia Institute of Marine Science; University of Washington; University of Wisconsin; Woods Hole Oceanographic Institution.

DIVING
ASSOCIATIONS &
PUBLICATIONS

ASSOCIATIONS

American Academy of
  Underwater Sciences
P.O. Box 12483
La Jolla, CA 92037–0645

California Wreck Divers
P.O. Box 9922
Marina Del Rey, CA 90291

Divers Alert Network (DAN)
Box 3823
Duke University Medical
  Center
Durham, NC 27710
(919) 684–2948 or
  (Emergency) (919) 684–8111

Diving Equipment
  Manufacturer's Association
  (DEMA)
P.O. Box 217
Tustin, CA 92680
(714) 730–0650

National Association of Cave
  Divers (NACD)
2900 Northwest 29th Avenue
Gainesville, FL 32605

National Association for Search
  & Recovery (NASAR)
P.O. Box 2123
La Jolla, CA 92038

National Oceanic and
   Atmospheric Administration
   (NOAA)
6010 Executive Boulevard
Rockville, MD 20852
(301) 443–8910

National Park Service
Southwest Region
P.O. Box 728
Santa Fe, NM 87501
(505) 476–1750

South Pacific Underwater
   Medical Society (SPUMS)
c / o Dr. Douglas Walker
P.O. Box 120
Narrabeen, NSW 2101
Australia

Undersea Explorers Society
   (UNEXSO)
P.O. Box F–2433
Freeport, Grand Bahama
(809) 373–1244

Undersea Medical Society
   (UMS)
9650 Rockville Pike
Bethesda, MD 20014
(301) 530–9225

Underwater Photographic
   Society (UPS)
P.O. Box 7088
Van Nuys, CA 91409

Underwater Society of America
(Dive Club Information)
238 Sunset
Glen Ellyn, IL 60137

PUBLICATIONS

Dive Industry News
PADI Headquarters
1243 East Warner Avenue
Santa Ana, CA 92705
(714) 540–7234

Diver
8051 River Road
Richmond, BC V6X 1X8
Canada
(604) 273–4333

*The Diving Retailer &
   Professional Instructor*
(A NASDS Publication)
P.O. Box 17067
Long Beach, CA 90807
(213) 595–5361

Diving & Snorkeling
Aqua-Field Publications
656 Shrewsbury Avenue
Suite One
Shrewsbury, NJ 07701
(201) 842–8300

The Dry Doc
(Publication of Human
   Underwater Biology, Inc.)
P.O. Box 5893
San Antonio, TX 78201
(512) 492–9395

Florida Scuba News
Wet Set Publications
1324 Placid Place
Jacksonville, FL 32205
(904) 384–7336

Pacific Diver
Seagraphic Publications Ltd.
1520 Alberni Street
Vancouver, BC,
Canada

Pipeline Industry
Gulf Publishing
P.O. Box 2608
Houston, TX 77001
(713) 529–4301

Scuba Times
P.O. Box 6268
Pensacola, FL 32503
(904) 478–5288

Skin Diver
(Petersen Publishing Co.)
8490 Sunset Boulevard
Los Angeles, CA 90069
(213) 657–5100

Undercurrent: The Private
  Exclusive Guide for Serious
  Divers
Atcom Building
2315 Broadway
New York, NY 10024
(212) 873–5900

The Undersea Journal
(PADI Publication)
1243 East Warner Avenue
Santa Ana, CA 92705
(714) 540–7234

Underwater USA
P.O. Box 705
Bloomsburg, PA 17815
(818) 784–6081

GLOSSARY

air embolism obstruction of blood vessels by gas bubbles. In diving, the term usually refers to those air bubbles entering the bloodstream, pumped by the heart to the brain.

bends *see* decompression sickness

bottom time the amount of time that elapses from the moment a diver leaves the surface to the time he begins to ascend—not just the amount of time spent at the lowest depth. Bottom time is important in establishing the amount of nitrogen the body absorbs during a dive.

buoyancy in water, the upward force exerted on a floating or immersed object

cylinder in diving terminology, a container holding compressed gas used for breathing underwater. *See also* tank.

DAN Divers Alert Network, a hot-line network designed to locate the necessary assistance during a dive emergency

decompression the release from pressure or compression. In diving, the term is used to describe the lessening of pressure on the body during ascent.

decompression sickness sometimes referred to as the bends. An injury or illness resulting from the formation of gas bubbles in the blood or tissues during, or following, an ascent and decompression.

dive tables This term usually refers to the U.S. Navy Standard Air Decompression Tables, which serve as a guide for preventing the accumulation of too much nitrogen by listing dive depths, bottom times, and rates of absorption.

diver down flags There are two recognized flags signifying that divers are in the vicinity. In the United States and Canada, the flag is a red square divided diagonally by a white bar. Elsewhere around the world, the flag recognized by the World Underwater Federation is "Flag Alpha"—the flag that represents the letter *A* in the International Code of Signals. This flag is square with a notch removed from the free edge. It is divided in half vertically; the mast half is white and the notched half is blue.

fins rubber devices that are attached to the feet to increase speed and facilitate motion underwater

hyperbaric chamber a metal vessel capable of being pressurized to simulate water depth. Sometimes called a decompression or recompression chamber, it is used primarily to treat decompression sickness.

mask a glass or plastic window surrounded by rubber, designed to fit against the face, providing air space between eyes and water. A regular diving mask covers nose and eyes only.

narcosis, or "rapture of the deep" a condition characterized by stupor or giddiness. In diving, mental impairment can range from a false sense of well-being to loss of consciousness.

regulator a device which, upon demand, delivers air into the diver's mouth

ROV remotely operated vehicle, an underwater robot

saturation, or SAT, diving a state in which the body's tissues have absorbed all the nitrogen or other inert gases they can hold at that particular depth

skin diving diving without the use of scuba

snorkel a J-shaped tube, the short end of which is held in the mouth, the long end protruding above the water to allow breathing without lifting one's nose out of the water

tank a hollow metal cylinder containing compressed air or gas used for breathing underwater. It is an integral part of scuba.

FURTHER READING

Earle, Sylvia, and Giddings, Al. *Exploring the Deep Frontier.* Washington, D.C.: National Geographic Society, 1980.

Empleman, Bernard. *The New Science of Skin and Scuba Diving.* Piscataway, N.J.: New Century, 1980.

McKenney, Jack. *Dive to Adventure.* Vancouver, British Columbia, Canada: Panorama Publications, 1983.

Miller, Manes. *NOAA Diving Manual,* 2nd ed. Washington, D.C.: U.S. Department of Commerce, 1979.

Settle, Mary Lee. *Water World.* New York: Lodestar Books, 1984.

Taylor, Herb. *The Sport Diving Catalog.* New York: St. Martin's Press, 1982.

INDEX

Page numbers in *italics* refer to illustrations.

ABOUT THE AUTHOR

Author Denise V. Lang is an avid scuba diver who has dived in many places around the world. One of her reasons for writing this book was "to entice others to leave the land behind and take a dive, entering an incredibly beautiful, colorful, and silent world that is there for us to enjoy."

Ms. Lang is a journalist, teacher, and lecturer. She has written for numerous specialty and national magazines, as well as Florida and New Jersey newspapers. Currently, she lives in Morristown, New Jersey, with her husband—who is also a scuba diver—and their two children.